Haunted Be the Holidays

Also from Heather Graham

Haunted Be the Holidays

A Krewe of Hunters Novella

By Heather Graham

1001 Dark Nights

EVIL EYE
CONCEPTS

Haunted Be the Holidays
A Krewe of Hunters Novella
Copyright 2018 Heather Graham Pozzessere
ISBN: 978-1-948050-21-0

Foreword: Copyright 2014 M. J. Rose

Published by Evil Eye Concepts, Incorporated

Haunted Be the Holidays

A Krewe of Hunters Novella

By Heather Graham

1001 Dark Nights

EVIL EYE
CONCEPTS

Haunted Be the Holidays
A Krewe of Hunters Novella
Copyright 2018 Heather Graham Pozzessere
ISBN: 978-1-948050-21-0

Foreword: Copyright 2014 M. J. Rose

Published by Evil Eye Concepts, Incorporated

Sign up for the 1001 Dark Nights Newsletter
and be entered to win a Tiffany Key necklace.

There's a contest every month!

Go to www.1001DarkNights.com

As a bonus, all subscribers will receive a free copy of
Discovery Bundle Three
Featuring stories by
Sidney Bristol, Darcy Burke, T. Gephart
Stacey Kennedy, Adriana Locke
JB Salsbury, and Erika Wilde

One Thousand and One Dark Nights

Once upon a time, in the future...

*I was a student fascinated with stories and learning.
I studied philosophy, poetry, history, the occult, and
the art and science of love and magic. I had a vast
library at my father's home and collected thousands
of volumes of fantastic tales.*

*I learned all about ancient races and bygone
times. About myths and legends and dreams of all
people through the millennium. And the more I read
the stronger my imagination grew until I discovered
that I was able to travel into the stories... to actually
become part of them.*

*I wish I could say that I listened to my teacher
and respected my gift, as I ought to have. If I had, I
would not be telling you this tale now.
But I was foolhardy and confused, showing off
with bravery.*

*One afternoon, curious about the myth of the
Arabian Nights, I traveled back to ancient Persia to
see for myself if it was true that every day Shahryar
(Persian: شهريار, "king") married a new virgin, and then
sent yesterday's wife to be beheaded. It was written
and I had read, that by the time he met Scheherazade,
the vizier's daughter, he'd killed one thousand
women.*

Something went wrong with my efforts. I arrived in the midst of the story and somehow exchanged places with Scheherazade – a phenomena that had never occurred before and that still to this day, I cannot explain.

Now I am trapped in that ancient past. I have taken on Scheherazade's life and the only way I can protect myself and stay alive is to do what she did to protect herself and stay alive.

Every night the King calls for me and listens as I spin tales. And when the evening ends and dawn breaks, I stop at a point that leaves him breathless and yearning for more. And so the King spares my life for one more day, so that he might hear the rest of my dark tale.

As soon as I finish a story... I begin a new one... like the one that you, dear reader, have before you now.

Something went wrong with my efforts. I arrived in the midst of the story and somehow exchanged places with Scheherazade – a phenomena that had never occurred before and that still to this day, I cannot explain.

Now I am trapped in that ancient past. I have taken on Scheherazade's life and the only way I can protect myself and stay alive is to do what she did to protect herself and stay alive.

Every night the King calls for me and listens as I spin tales. And when the evening ends and dawn breaks, I stop at a point that leaves him breathless and yearning for more. And so the King spares my life for one more day, so that he might hear the rest of my dark tale.

As soon as I finish a story... I begin a new one... like the one that you, dear reader, have before you now.

Prologue

Washington, D.C.
October 1867
All Saints' Eve

"It will be grand—incredibly grand!" Judson Newby said. "Can you imagine, the lights, the elegance—society decked out in splendor. And all to see you, my love! And, of course, I've checked with the priests in the district and northern Virginia—I've made sure that our curtain will coincide nicely with the last masses and services for the eve of All Saints' Day."

He grinned, shaking his head. "Some people…well, they might have visited the graves of their loved ones or be planning on doing so tomorrow. So many Irish in this city, bringing their bit about Celtic lore with them, thinking the dead rise on All Hallows' Eve. Be that as it may, they visit the dead by day—and church services will be over in plenty of time for them all to make the eight-thirty curtain."

Listening to him, Caroline Hartford smiled, loving his enthusiasm. She was still amazed by the fact that Judson had chosen her, and that soon they would be married.

And, perhaps most amazing of all, he was happy about her love for the theater and her longing to perform. Many men would demand that she quit—but not Judson. The hero of many a Civil War battle, he remained a respected and beloved character in D.C., and the capital city was enjoying a tremendous growth boom.

D.C. had been founded by none other than President Washington in 1790 and given over to Pierre L'Enfant for design. And it had been beautifully planned.

But it had also taken many blows. The War of 1812 had seen much of the city burned to the ground. The grand boulevards of L'Enfant's Paris-style vision had taken a brutal beating. But now another war—a war that had shaken and tested a nation—was over and people wanted work. They wanted a new beginning—and many of those people were flocking to the city. Some who came were burnt and broken themselves, seeking a haven and the opportunity to rise again, and D.C. was known to provide both.

Others were counting on that boom as they crawled higher and higher in politics and society.

They were creating the right kind of audience for a sound theatrical existence.

For a time, people had feared the theater—after all, Lincoln had been assassinated at Ford's Theater.

But then again, the martyred president had loved theater—and thus, so should they all.

She felt another tremor of amazement and gratitude. Judson was the finest man she had ever met—and he loved her. She was certain. And though he had not told her that he was either the owner of the theater or had invested heavily in it – she knew that it was because of his involvement that it had survived and was beginning to thrive.

It had been owned once, but that owner had disappeared, died, or simply defaulted. It had since gone to ruin, and she had remarked on the fact one day. Soon after, repairs on the slowly decaying beauty had begun, and here she was. And…

She knew inside that Judson had bought it.

For her.

Even on All Hallows' Eve, their opening, she just knew, would be wonderful.

In honor of the Celtic concept of the holiday, perhaps—and perhaps to draw large audiences who loved a touch of the gruesome and frightening, but only at a distance—they would open with a brand-new take on Mary Shelley's classic of *Frankenstein, or the Modern Prometheus*—with Caroline performing the role of the doctor's fiancée. An unbelievable song had been written for her, a lovely lament that came at the climax of the play. Their version of the classic was called

The Rising of Monsters and Men.

Judson would be there, front row, proudly clapping his beloved on.

Of course, the opening had been set before they had realized the date—All Hallows' Eve, or All Saints' Day Eve. They had never meant to be disrespectful, and of course, Judson had talked to all the priests and pastors he knew.

If a grand opening didn't hamper services, all was fine.

And, to placate the Irish and those of Celtic backgrounds, Judson had studied Jack-O-Lanterns. Apparently, some unlucky fellow named Jack had made a deal with the devil and was forced to walk around some kind of purgatory in the dark...so he had to carry a turnip with a candle to keep the darkness at bay.

There would be carved lanterns in the lobby as theater-goers entered.

Everything was covered. Because of Judson.

Life was amazing.

They stood before the stage, Caroline and her beloved Judson, just admiring the work of the stagecraft team. The set was perfect, the lighting having been carefully crafted. The orchestra was excellent, and she knew she had been gifted with a sweet and clear voice, one that would fill the grand cavern of the theater.

And yet, something dark seemed to slip over her, casting a chill like a rush of cold water through her veins.

She shivered suddenly.

"What is it, my love?" Judson asked.

"I don't know," she said, confused. "I felt...as if there were footsteps over my grave, as if...I don't know. As if something cold touched me."

"There is nothing cold here," he told her, pulling her close. "There is only the warmth of me. The fire of all that lives between us, of the lives we will live, in love forever."

She stared up at him, wonder in her eyes. "That you should love me..."

It was amazing. She had grown up in the poorest of conditions, shuffled from orphanage to orphanage, finally landing on the footsteps of a house sold to Ronald Colby—owner of a theater. She had cleaned, she had pressed costumes, she had worked and worked...and in doing so, she had befriended glittering stars, music masters, and more. And one day, Colby had realized the little orphan he had rescued had gained, on her own, a greater value. She was known in the city as "The Lark." She didn't fight the moniker—it was a good one to have.

"No," Judson said. "That you should love me," he whispered.

Amazing…so amazing. Tonight would be glorious. And after that, her life…

With Judson…

More than anyone dared dream.

"So dinner, my beloved, and then back to costume and makeup— and the grand opening!"

"Just one moment," she told him. "I must get my reticule."

She left him there, staring at the stage, and hurried up the sides to the apron and then on back to the left wing.

Hurry—dinner! She reminded herself.

She walked quickly around to the stairs that led down to the dressing, preparation, and storage rooms.

Only one lamp was lit. There was no reason for more until the stage manager came in and the cast and the crew and the flurry preceding the show began. She'd had a gas lamp earlier at her dressing table, but she hadn't kept it lit. Theater was still an expensive proposal, and if they didn't do well…money would always be an object.

Caroline walked down the hallway where doors opened into dressing rooms, storage, prop, and costume rooms. She had grown into one of the company's stars and had her own dressing room near the stairs, allowing for quick costume changes when need be.

On the way, she noticed the prop room door was ajar. She paused to close it and was startled by a leering face. She laughed softy to herself because it was the mask used by the monster in the show. In this twist on the original story, the horror of the creature only showed at certain times. And when it did, there was no time to transform the actor on stage.

The mask, conceived to look like a death's head, made its appearance in the second act. It was horrible, created as a skeletal face with narrow bones, huge black eyes and a gaping mouth that twisted into a leering scowl.

She'd seen the mask at dress rehearsal, but it was still a chilling sight. It was set atop a stand that had been draped with the monster's cloak, and it appeared to be as real as possible—without an actor even wearing it.

"You scared me!" she told the mask.

And closed the door.

Despite the lack of light here now, it was easy enough to feel her way to her dressing table in her small—but oh, so special and appreciated—dressing room. And even to find her little bag. She knew exactly where she'd left it. She grabbed her reticule, hurried out and paused—the prop room door was ajar again. The leering death's head was sticking out at an odd angle.

Something had to be wrong with the way the thing had been set.

Sighing, she started to walk back to the room and see what the difficulty could be.

The face on the thing was cruel and menacing.

"Quite frightening," she told the piece, approaching it.

"Caroline."

She froze. It had seemed to say her name. Fear spread through her with a vengeance.

It would have to remain as it was, she decided. She was not staying a minute longer and Judson was right upstairs.

She turned to walk away and wound up running.

But as she reached the stairs and started up them, she knew that someone or *something* was behind her. She turned, compelled by some unknown force.

And she was stunned to see that the *thing,* the horrible mask, worn by *someone* who had also donned the cloak, was there before her.

She started to let out a scream.

It never left her lips. The thing came after her, seeming to float up the stairs, black cloaked arms flying...

Encompassing her and whispering before she could scream.

"The theater is mine, don't you understand? The theater will always be mine."

Its arms tightened as she choked out a dying, muted cry for help.

But she was silenced.

Forever.

Chapter 1

Washington, D.C.
Halloween
Now

"It's trick or treat, trick or treat!"

A tiny creature—a boy? Of maybe five? —rushed in front of Dakota "Kody" McCoy as she walked quickly down the street. Hard to tell the sex of the child as he—or she—was wearing a costume that resembled a grinning, walking shark. Very clever, and most probably homemade.

"Trick or treat? Yes, trick or treat!" she said, wishing she had thought to carry some candy on her.

Another child—a bit bigger, this one wearing a mermaid costume and sporting a full head of naturally red hair—joined the "shark."

"Trick or treat!" the little girl said.

The parents weren't far behind, and they were equally well-decked for the holiday as Frankenstein and the Bride of Frankenstein.

"I'm so sorry!" the mother said, catching up with her children. "Darlings, we don't trick or treat the people who are out walking."

"It's fine, it's fine," Kody assured her. "I'm just so sorry—I don't have candy. Wait, I do have quarters—for a game room." She remembered her last visit to a game room and hastily amended her words. "Bills, bills for the game room."

She reached into her shoulder bag for her wallet. Both the mom and dad protested, but Kody assured them that she was delighted by the children, they had made her day. She slipped a dollar into the pumpkin baskets they carried and wished them a happy Halloween.

She smiled as she again hurried along the street, glancing at her watch as she did so.

She was early. There was no real reason for her to rush, but she was anxious to reach the old Global Tower Theater - Adam Harrison's refurbished find just blocks from Union Station in the heart of the capitol.

She felt a little guilty that no one would be at the house she and Brodie McFadden had rented in a gated community in Alexandria. Their little conclave was family oriented, and there would be no one there to give out candy. While Brodie had yet to go through his class at the FBI Academy to officially become part of the Krewe, he—and his older brothers, Bryan and Bruce—were still on the payroll as "consultants." He'd been supposed to be with her here, now, seeing the children's show and the night show. But Jackson had called him—and she had urged him to go and help out with whatever it was that was going on.

Jackson Crow was the field head of the Krewe of Hunters—not to mention an amazing man.

And she really didn't mind. Brodie, being incredibly supportive of her work with the theater, had already seen both shows several times.

That made her smile. She still couldn't believe sometimes that life had brought her here—with Brodie.

He was incredibly supportive in every way. Even though it seemed he groaned his way through the Halloween season while she loved it.

Now, he'd told her he could think of some pretty good costumes for her—very different from the staid Victorian clothing she'd wear that night for the mainstage adult performance.

Then again, he liked her without costumes at all, without...

She shook her head, happy at the wealth of Halloween confusion around her.

The sun had risen beautifully, and the day stayed clear with the early fall afternoon offering a pleasant feel--the temperature was hovering right at 70 degrees. Tonight, for the children of the District of Columbia, it would drop no lower than 60-plus—perfect weather for costumes and parties and Halloween trick-or-treating.

And this early evening—in time to change around for the

nighttime, adult performance--her production for the children's division of the theater, a play she'd written herself entitled *Things That Go Bump in the Night,* would end its run.

Then the fall shows, leading up to Thanksgiving, would begin. Followed by the Christmas shows.

As far as this children's theater production, Kody had been given free rein.

That she had such an incredible and historic theater with which to become involved was amazing from the get-go. Some of the greatest men and women in American history had enjoyed performances here—Jenny Lind had sung here. But despite a fight on many ends to preserve the old theater, its condition had been so poor that even preservation boards had been about to give up on it.

Enter Adam Harrison, a philanthropist and the founder of the Krewe of Hunters. He heard about the theater and its longevity, and it became one of his pet projects. Adam had pulled together the resources needed to repair and preserve the building.

Kody was not the first with a Krewe association to become part of the theater. Adam had hired other actors who were significant others in one way or another to Krewe members. Alexi Cromwell, who was now married to Special Agent Jude McCoy – who shared Kody's last name but was no relation to her – was the first to be hired on. She had been working as a piano-bar hostess on an historic ship when she'd met Jude and Adam, who were on a case. Next, Adam had brought in Clara Avery, wife of Special Agent Thor Erikson, who'd worked on a television show. And then Charlene Moreau, who had been doing well in movies and all aspects of acting, was now engaged to Special Agent Ethan Delaney. Charlene and Ethan had known each other years before when they'd both lived in the St. Francisville area of Louisiana. And just a year or so ago, she'd become involved in a case with Ethan when she had been filming in northern Louisiana. Then there was Marnie Davante, now married to the man who would be Kody's brother-in-law, Brodie's oldest brother, Bryan. She smiled, thinking that Bruce—the middle brother in the McFadden family— had told her that his fiancée, Sophie Manning, was going into the Academy along with him.

Sophie had been a detective out in L.A. And, of course, she was perfect for the Krewe. She'd easily passed all requirements to get into the Academy, then from there into the Krewe. But Sophie was a fan of the theater as well. And like many other Krewe members and significant others, she supported this one whole-heartedly.

Alexi Cromwell was the artistic director of the theater—and made the final decisions.

Clara Avery was in charge of musical theater operations. Charlene—or Charlie—headed up the adult division, choosing the shows they would do, obtaining rights, and so on. All three of them worked on casting and directing shows.

Kody had come from a background as a curator and owned her own small museum in Key West. It wasn't that she hadn't been on several stages before—just in a different capacity. And when Marnie had left with Bryan for a seminar on criminal profiling, she had been happy to take over Marnie's love—the children's theater. She'd found herself fascinated and ready to pitch in wherever she was needed. And after this busy season was over, she planned on truly diving into the incredible history of the place.

To her surprise, she'd been cast for the leading role in the Halloween season's adult show. She still wasn't sure why. The others were immensely talented—and certainly able. But Charlie had planned on being gone for most of the season, and she'd assured Kody that the beauty of the operation was the fact they were a true ensemble group—able to fill in for one another in just about any position at any time.

Kody had something else in her background that made it possible for her to step in so easily. Her father had been a mega-popular rock star, Michael McCoy of the Bone Island Boys. She'd known music from the time she'd been born. She'd loved her father and had performed with him many a time, not to mention that in his later years, he'd been involved with special performances and fundraisers to support several local theater projects in the Keys.

Kody had naturally been a part of them all. She'd adored her father. Not that he'd always been a nice guy, but she knew that marriage to her mother—and the life he'd lived as a father—had changed him. He'd lived clean, his outbursts had ceased, and the world had seen an obnoxious and entitled man become a sober and giving icon.

She smiled. It was nice to think that she'd been part of that change.

Now she worked with a board of amazing women, who together managed all aspects and who had been enthusiastic to welcome Kody in.

She still needed to get back to Key West now and again. But that was the beauty of them all being able to slip into one another's shoes whenever necessary.

The theater gave work to many people not associated with the Krewe, and it also afforded outlets for other Krewe members at times. The creation of the Krewe was equally fascinating to Kody. Krewe members had come from all walks of life before applying to the Academy, making their way through it, and then joining the special unit. Will Chan—a magician and tech wizard before joining the Krewe—sometimes gave a special performance.

Plus--even with all of them working and running the place, they had a little *extra* assistance—whether they wanted it or not.

Kody had quickly become very familiar with that…assistance.

She smiled, thinking about Maeve and Hamish McFadden. She had been enamored of the acting duo as a child. And now…

Now Kody was engaged to their youngest son, Brodie, who was working as a "consultant" for the Krewe while awaiting his class at the FBI Academy. And she was here—discovering she loved producing and directing children's theater—and performing in musicals herself.

Naturally, it was always a bit traumatic to meet someone— especially during a murder investigation—fall in love, and then meet the parents.

Meeting Maeve and Hamish McFadden had given new meaning to getting accustomed to the prospective in-laws—since the two were dead.

Although the McFaddens had been renowned for their performances in many epic movies, they had both loved the theater. They had perished together during a show—luckily, not at this theater.

But that didn't keep them from wanting to help run it.

Kody did get to help run the children's division—and she loved it.

Things That Go Bump in the Night ran for seventy minutes plus intermission. This afternoon's production started at three-thirty and ended at five. That allowed for her young actors to change and clear out, sets and costumes to be switched, and for the performers to arrive

and prepare for the adult performance, which started at eight.

She often remained at the theater, even when the children were finished, to help out with the night shows. This season, she'd even accepted a role in the adult show—*The Rising of Monsters and Men*, loosely based on the Mary Shelley classic *Frankenstein*.

It was a fitting show for Halloween—even if the first leading lady to rehearse the role had died before her opening night, having taken a tumble down the stairs that led to the costume, prop, lighting, and dressing rooms that were in the basement.

It had all been redone, of course. The stairs—once dangerous—were safer by far, and the rooms now included a set-design studio as well.

The ghost of Caroline Hartford, the poor, beautiful, ill-fated young lady, was said to haunt the theater.

Kody had never seen her. Neither had Maeve or Hamish, who assured her that if a spirit presence was around, they would certainly know.

If Caroline Hartford was haunting the theater, Judson Newby should be haunting it, too. The then-owner of the theater and a strapping man in his mid-thirties at the time, had perished himself in the theater, his heart giving out when he found his beloved at the foot of the stairs.

A double reason, the ghost of Hamish McFadden had told her, for the residential ghosts of the theater to have been the ill-fated couple.

But, apparently, while ghost books published by just about every travel writer and ghost "expert" in the country claimed that the two haunted the place, they certainly hadn't shown themselves to anyone Kody knew—living or dead.

Her phone rang, and she glanced at the caller I.D. before answering it quickly. It was Charly Atwood, who managed the box office.

"Hey, Charly," she said.

"Hey Kody, I just wanted to let you know—we have a full house for our performance this afternoon. We'd been down to a few seats…but I called around and did a little shuffling so people desperate for a pair of tickets might sit together." He laughed softly. "Seriously, how many theaters would offer that kind of help?"

"Oh, Charly, that's wonderful. Thank you so much. I'm almost there. Just coming down the street."

"I didn't call to rush you. Just to let you know. Ginny is here already, checking costumes, and Percy is working on set. Everything is going great."

"Thank you so much. I'm almost there anyway. See you soon. And thank you again. That is above and beyond the call of duty."

"A labor of love," he assured her, and hung up.

Charly Atwood was an amazing man. He'd worked at the theater twenty years ago, before it had been abandoned—for the third or fourth time in its history—for lack of funds and enthusiasm. There were several box office employees, of course, but Charly managed it all and was amazing at numbers and keeping sales going—even arranging for rearranging what had already been purchased.

Ginny Granger, wardrobe mistress, was equally wonderful. She'd worked several years on Broadway and could keep up with costumes like no one else. And Percy Ainsworth was just about magic—he had a heck of a history, having been on stage himself years before, and made his way up through the ranks with his stagecraft. A gifted man, he managed all areas—props, building, breaking down, saving—he could change sets, repair sets, and even build a new set in the blink of an eye.

She was grateful for them all.

Nearing the theater, she paused, surprised to discover she was…

Looking for ghosts.

Well, there certainly weren't any to be seen. What she did see was more children—scores of children. Big ones, little ones—all out for candy. It was Halloween, after all. They were in costumes. Moms and dads or uncles, aunts, cousins, or friends walked with them, sometimes in costume, and sometimes not.

No other little munchkins ran up to her for treats, but they were an entertaining sight.

Yep, it was Halloween.

Kody loved costumes—maybe it was part of loving the theater.

And that was why she immediately noticed the death's head costume.

It was eerily similar to the one that had been designed for their play.

The costume's mask resembled a death's head on a seventeenth-century tombstone. The mouth gaped open, and the figure was wearing—as all evil characters seemed to sport—a black cape and hood.

The "death's head" character spun around on the street, delighting kids as they scurried away.

It did a little dance on the sidewalk right in front of Kody, and the performance was a good one—the costume wearer could dance. He or she was doing a big *à la* Michael Jackson number, well timed and compelling, even with the cape on.

Only a Fedora was needed to make it complete.

Kody hadn't realized she had paused to watch—until the end of the performance.

Then the character—with its gaping-mouth death's head mask—came to a stop. People on the street started to applaud. Kody did the same.

Then it turned to her, slowly, theatrically, as if knowing she—specifically—was there.

It bowed deeply, rose, looked at her a long moment, and then walked off into the crowd.

Kody gave herself a serious mental shake as a wave of coldness ran through her body. She wasn't easily frightened, and she didn't know what it was about the performance that had disturbed her. Everyone around her was clapping. And it was Halloween. It was ridiculous to be afraid of a costumed performer on Halloween.

Except, of course, tonight she was in a show featuring a very similar figure. An evil being out to kidnap and kill her character.

Was that it?

Enough. Her children's theater's last production of the Halloween show was coming up, and all the costumed characters were filled with fun and made children laugh.

Her own performance in the night's production would follow quickly. She needed to move. Forget the strange dance she had just seen—better yet, appreciate it for what it had been, a charming dance by an adult who loved Halloween and wanted to entertain those on the street.

She hurried on toward the theater.

But the strange chill that had invaded her remained.

* * * *

A shelf full of grisly masks sat to Brodie McFadden's right, along with zombie costumes—still popular and in high demand—and hanging skeletons and little witches' cauldrons, guaranteed to stir up some fog with just "a tiny drop of water."

At the end of the aisle was a blood-soaked creature wielding a hatchet. It had a sign that promised, "Guaranteed to scare the pants off your friends! Motion-activated!"

Brodie shook his head, turning to his left.

These shelves boasted dancing reindeer, a plastic, laughing Santa, ornaments in every color of the rainbow, and a section devoted to different Menorahs.

It was Halloween—and already, Christmas ornaments and décor were flowing over the shelves.

Brodie took a moment to note the discrepancy of the offerings, and then turned back to the anxious young clerk, Rebecca Cameron, who stood in front of him.

"Okay," he said gently. "You're convinced the blood was real?"

"You don't believe me!" she said indignantly.

"No, I believe you. I just want you to think carefully. It *is* Halloween. You don't think the young woman was in costume, or the blood might have been faked?" he asked.

The clerk was about twenty-four years old, tiny in height, dark-eyed and dark-haired, with a round, friendly face. Right now, however, her eyes were large, pupils dilated, and she appeared to be frightened.

"Mr. McFadden," she said. "I'm telling you, I've worked here since I got out of high school. I...I know kids at Halloween—and *adults* at Halloween. This woman...she was crazed. I think she...that she—she ate someone, somewhere."

"Ate them?" he asked carefully.

"Or drained them of blood. I could smell blood on her—it had that rusting tin kind of smell..."

He did know the smell. He might be a consultant at the moment, and not officially a Krewe agent yet, but he'd been military, he'd been a private eye—and, unfortunately, he'd already been on more than a few murder investigations.

"Oh, I don't know—she ate someone—someone munched on her neck. There was just so much blood."

"It could have been fake," he said gently.

"Not unless she ordered some 'Eau de Blood' to go with it! I know costumes and makeup. We're right by the theater, and," she added dryly, "I have witnessed Halloween all my life. And at Halloween, there are always people running around in costume—and not just the players. But this…this was real blood."

"All right, you said she was covered in blood. And it could have been hers. Could she have been hurt somehow?" Brodie asked. "Was there any kind of an injury you could see?"

"Oh, God!" the young clerk said. "I don't know. Maybe. Maybe she was in real pain. But she was obnoxious—threatening. She wanted opioids. Yes, I mean, I guess that would mean she might be hurt. Her neck was all red—but the blood was all over the costume, too. At a distance, I thought maybe she was doing a just-enjoyed-dinner vampire or something. But when she got closer…there was that smell!"

"And when she got belligerent at the pharmacy counter, you heard her—and walked up and warned her you were going to call the police?" Brodie asked.

Rebecca nodded solemnly.

He glanced quickly at the notes on his cellphone. The woman was young, but as she said, she'd been there several years. She was a clerk, and an assistant store manager, and she had called in the incident— which might have been a non-incident, not something that would normally involve the FBI.

Except Detective Angus Hilton of the D.C. police was close friends with Jackson Crow, head of the Krewe unit of the bureau. Since Brodie had just picked up Jackson to head to the theater—all who could were gathering for the last children's and adult Halloween season shows—he had found himself investigating what might have been an addict's attempt to fulfill a craving.

Halloween—like a full moon—brought out the crazies.

But there had been a rash of disappearances in the District of Columbia and surrounding areas, which meant Angus had asked Jackson for help. And, while Brodie spoke with the clerk, Jackson was talking to Angus, getting a better grip on the detective's concerns.

Inwardly, he sighed.

It was supposed to have been a great afternoon and a good night.

Of course, it would still be a good night and a good afternoon, he was certain. When they finished up here, they'd head for the theater.

No, no they wouldn't, he admitted to himself. Not until they had done some investigating themselves, no matter how many law enforcement officers were out on the streets, ready for the craziness of Halloween.

He glanced quickly across rows of paper towels, plastic cups, and dish detergent. Jackson and Angus were by the front door. A young stock boy was showing them how the bloody woman had run from the store when she'd found out the police were coming.

"Mr. McFadden," the clerk told him, "Please believe me. Someone out there is…bleeding—or they made someone else bleed, and they might do it again. Yes, someone out there is definitely bleeding."

And possibly dead or dying, he thought.

"We'll find her—and find out what happened," he assured her. "I believe Detective Hilton will want you to go with him to the station to work with a sketch artist. Will that be a problem for you?"

She shook her head. "This is an independent pharmacy and store," she told him. "We've already put up signs apologizing for being closed and giving people a number to call for emergency pharmacy needs. I'm happy to help him. There was something so…wrong about the woman."

"Thank you," Brodie told her. "And excuse me. An officer will be right with you."

He headed toward the front of the store where Angus and Jackson waited.

They were now standing by a display rack that contained Halloween candy in skeleton form—and chocolate reindeer.

Angus Hilton was fifty-five, with steely gray hair, steady powder-blue eyes, and a gaunt, somewhat world-weary face.

Perhaps his look of weariness was not a surprise—he'd worked in D.C. for twenty years.

The detective noted the way that he was glancing at the sales rack with the oddly mismatched candy.

"Hey, we're a capitalist society—you have to make money when making money is good," he said dryly. "Nothing like some cute little chocolate reindeers to go with skeletons." He paused, shaking his head, a look of perplexity on his face.

"What is it?" Jackson asked.

"No turkeys," Hilton said.

"Turkeys?"

Hilton gave himself a little shake. "Sorry—no turkeys. No cute little turkeys—it's going right from Halloween to Christmas."

"Maybe there will be turkeys when the skeletons are cleared out," Brodie told him. "I've been speaking with Miss Cameron."

"Yes, yes, and thank you. What was your take on her distress? Is she just an alarmist—or do you think we have a body or a killer or both out there somewhere?"

"I believe her distress is real. What did the others say?" Brodie asked.

"The stock boy was still shaking," Jackson said. "There was something—something real and worth investigating."

"What do you say, Brodie?"

"I do believe that somewhere out there, a woman with a bloodied face is running around. Miss Cameron is happy to work with a sketch artist. That might help us. Whether she's dangerous to others or a victim isn't clear. We have to find her, though."

"Yes, thank you. I'll have a patrolman get her to the station right away and we'll get a sketch out, add it to the other information I've sent out already," Hilton said. "Local cops are searching." He sighed. "So this is what we know. She ran back out the front door here—Jackson and I have been looking for any sign of blood drops—nothing so far. But I've got a forensic team coming out. I'm sorry for calling you guys. It just sounded…well, up your alley. They do call you guys the 'weird-stuff squad,' along with 'ghostbusters' and a few other things. All respectfully, of course."

"Hey, whatever," Jackson said casually. "And, my friend, you've helped the Krewe out often enough with information and man power in the area, so…no problem."

Hilton glanced back toward Rebecca Cameron. "You know, I think I'll take her down myself to get a sketch going." He hesitated. "I really wouldn't have dragged you in on this, except…three people missing, and each time our officers investigated…there were strange blood drops. They belonged to the men and women who were missing, and they might have been from a cut or a minor accident. No blood baths—just specs of blood. So when she said this woman was covered in blood…"

"We'll need the files on the missing—anything you have," Jackson told him.

"Of course." Hilton looked at Brodie. "The clerk—Miss Rebecca Cameron...she doesn't come off as just crazy as all hell, right?"

"No. She believes something is very wrong. Now, whether this woman was really covered in someone's blood or not, I don't know. The opioid problem, as we all know, is out of control. She might have been a dressed-up addict. But what makes me think the woman who came in here was covered in real blood was that Rebecca Cameron said she *smelled* that tinny smell that goes with real blood. So..."

"So we'll all be out looking for a messy-eating vampire. On Halloween," Hilton said wearily.

Brodie nodded grimly and looked at Jackson.

"Or a person dressed up as a vampire attacked by someone else," he said. "We'll get on the local area here—it is Halloween. I'd hate for a young child to come upon her...or her to come upon a young child."

Jackson Crow seldom betrayed his thoughts. Half Native American, he had a powerful, striking lean face with high cheekbones and level eyes.

He nodded as Brodie spoke.

So much for the theater that afternoon.

Maybe the night could be salvaged.

He doubted it. He had an uneasy feeling.

Maybe it was just Halloween.

Somehow, he doubted that, too.

Chapter 2

There were three ten-year-old children performing in *Things That Go Bump in the Night,* and three adults.

The kids were great. Robert Appleby, playing the oldest brother, had been seen by a talent scout and offered a role in a movie about to be made from a popular series of young adult novels. He loved acting, and was grateful to her for casting him. And his energy for the show had infused all her performers.

It was also the last show.

The "things that went bump in the night" in the show all proved to be benign. The play went through common fears—darkness, kids' closets, and of course, the possibility of a monster beneath the bed. At the end of the show, Kody always gave a little speech, often inviting in an officer from either the D.C. police or from the neighboring communities in northern Virginia or Maryland to join her.

That day, Officer England from the Arlington police came in and gave the kids a safety speech. While many things were childhood fears, there were also bad things in life, and kids needed to be kids—but be smart and careful as well.

He was wonderful, and they ended the children's portion of the day with Kody thanking him and her cast and all those who had supported her.

Kody tended to disappear as quickly as possible from the stage. There were always people in the audience who remembered the few times she had performed with her father years before. She liked people, and she was happy to give out autographs or have pictures taken, but at the theater, when she was doing double duty, there just wasn't time. At least not until after the main stage show.

The children filed out. Even as they left, the crew, actors, and stage manager—Clara Avery having taken that position for the run of the show, despite her usual run as a show's soprano and leading lady—walked in.

Kody was picking up one of the stuffed dogs used by the "Smith" children in the play when Clara reached her, giving her a quick hug.

"Hey," Kody told her friend and co-worker. "Boy, you are right on time!"

"Nope—I've been here. Alexi is out front, talking to one of the ushers. We both came to see the last performance of your first show here."

"Oh, so nice of you guys. And, hey—the kids' theater is really Marnie's—"

"I'm sure you'll do more shows," Clara said.

Kody smiled her gratitude. Clara was an exceptionally attractive woman with a quick smile and a love for life that made her more so. She was also an amazing soprano—but the score for this show had been written for a lower voice range—something she could have handled fine, but it was a role truly suited to Kody.

"Hey, this place is incredibly cool for all of us—and so much so for me."

"We do well, don't we?" Clara said. "I saw Angela Hawkins in the audience, too, but I didn't get a chance to talk to her. She went running out at the end, and—though she manages to be polite and discreet in a theater—I think she was looking at something on her phone. So, since she handles the case load, I'm thinking something happened and she had to head back to work to decide if it was a Krewe case, and if so, who to send where." Clara shrugged. "I—I didn't see Brodie."

"Yeah, I don't know what happened. He was supposed to be here. I haven't had a chance to call him or even check my phone. I'll do that now."

Kody headed back to the stage-left wing where she'd left her shoulder bag draped over one of the Victorian chairs ready to come out for the night show set.

As she walked, Clara called after her, "Hey, did you see the performer outside? He might give us a run for our money tonight!"

Kody wasn't at all sure why, but Clara's words sent a shiver racing down her spine. She stopped and turned back.

"A performer outside? Was he wearing a something like a death's head mask—similar to the one in the play?"

"Yeah. I hadn't thought about it, but, yes, it's kind of similar. It's getting crazy busy out there. Kids galore—with parents. And just people dressed up. Everyone stopped for this guy though. A hell of a dancer."

Kody forgot about her bag. She hurried back to the stage and rushed down the stairs, heading along a velvet-carpeted aisle to reach the lobby.

"Kody!"

Charly was behind the glassed-in box-office area, looking dapper in his tux. He kept his hair long, and by his appearance might have been a dressed-up and slightly aged rocker from the eighties.

"Yes?"

Courtesy caused her to pause for a minute. And smile.

"Sold out for tonight's performance, too—you go, girl!"

"Thanks, Charly!" she said and burst out to the sidewalk beyond the theater.

The performer was gone. She walked up and down, but she didn't see him.

Walking back, she frowned.

There were drops of blood on the sidewalk, leading from the corner…

Right up to the door of the theater.

Then they stopped, as if whatever had been dripping that blood had simply vanished into thin air.

* * * *

"Halloween."

Jackson said the word wearily.

"You know," he continued, "when I was a kid, I loved the holiday beyond imagination. Now, now that I've been where I've been, seen what I've seen, and in heading up the Krewe…"

Halloween spelled trouble, and Brodie McFadden knew it well. There was something about a plethora of jack-o-lanterns, movie monsters, front-lawn-graveyards, ghosts, ghouls, and goblins that seemed to bring out the devious machinations of the most heinous criminals.

"It's because it's a wonderful night to hide in plain sight," Brodie said.

They had already walked several miles around the area.

They'd paused to talk to several "vampires."

None proved to be covered in real blood.

Halloween might have been better celebrated at malls or neighborhoods—or at house parties. But no matter how many venues offered special events and candy, people still took to the streets.

"Looking for a needle in a haystack," he murmured.

Of course, every patrol officer out there tonight had been warned to be on the lookout for the woman who had come into the pharmacy. And yet, despite his belief in Rebecca Cameron's certainty, they might just be on a wild goose chase.

Yes, looking for a needle in a haystack.

"Maybe I should go this alone. You can head to the theater—"

"No, and Kody will understand," Brodie said. He paused for a moment, looking at Jackson. "Hey, who knows? Maybe we'll turn a corner and find this woman."

"Doubtful," Jackson said.

They turned a corner.

They were about five blocks from the pharmacy—almost as if they were at the point of a perfect triangle from both the pharmacy and the theater.

They had come upon the Anderson House, a beautiful old mansion built about a decade after the White House, but still privately owned. Herbert Iberville, who owned it now, had made a fortune producing and directing music videos, and as such, he loved anything theatrical.

The yard had been done up amazingly for the holiday—both sides of the sloping lawn had become part of a cemetery with monsters having a graveyard bash.

Music played. "I See a Bad Moon Rising" ended and "Monster Mash" began as they paused in front of the house.

Kids were hurrying up the long walkway to the antebellum-style porch, where candy was being given out. "We'll head on up and ask them if they've seen anything--unusual," Jackson said.

"Wait," Brodie murmured.

He was looking to the left. Haphazard Styrofoam gravestones littered the yard with pumpkin-headed scarecrows, zombies, monsters, witches and more interspersed between them.

Some zombies were crawling out of the ground. A green witch sat on a tomb sipping tea and speaking with a mummy.

The work in the yard was phenomenal, and the owner had evidently created it with a great love for set design and the holiday. It was fantastic, but there was just one thing that seemed oddly out of place.

Not out of place…

It was a vampire. A female vampire. But she wasn't chatting with the other fabrications.

She was lying wide-eyed between a few of the tombs.

He headed off the path and to the side of the yard.

Before he even reached the vampire, he smelled it.

The tinny smell of blood, mixed with the smell of death.

Without turning around, he lifted a hand to Jackson, who quickly followed in his wake. The yard was on a slope; he strode up it past all manner of the creations and came to the woman. Down on his knees, he studied her.

Blood was all around her mouth. It dotted the crimson dress she wore in dark stains and clotted on her black cape.

Jackson hunched down beside him, his cell phone out as he called it in.

Hide in plain sight.

Looking down at the corpse, he wondered just how long the thing had been hidden in plain sight.

And was this the "vampire" who had walked into the pharmacy?

He didn't touch the corpse. That was the medical examiner's duty. He studied what he could see. Pinpoint pricks on her neck—real or drawn-on. Bright red lipstick, dark eyes…she had been in her mid to late twenties. Medium height, medium build. Nails long and sharpened to points.

Patrol officers arrived quickly, creating a perimeter.

Trick-or-treating was over for the night at Anderson House. Kids were filing out.

Brodie stood and waited, watching to make sure none of the revelers stepped past the yellow crime scene tape.

"Hey, mister! Way to ruin Halloween!" a boy in a "Walking Dead" outfit called to him.

"Yep, way to ruin it. Sorry," Brodie said.

An older kid at the boy's side nudged him, looking up at Brodie. He looked scared—as if Brodie was the most frightening thing he'd seen all night.

"FBI," he murmured.

"Yes, and sorry, kid. Truly, I'm sorry."

And so, I'm sure, is she, he added silently as the kids moved away.

Without the costume, she'd been young and lovely.

And now she was young, and lovely, and dead.

Suddenly, with no sound reason, Brodie worried about Kody. She would, of course, understand why he wasn't there at the theater. He didn't like not being there—now. Because there was a killer out there. Someone who could hide in plain sight, and even hide his victims in plain sight.

It was Halloween.

But…

She was in a theater.

As he thought of her, his phone rang.

It was Kody.

He tried to keep any fear out of his voice as he answered, quickly apologizing, explaining the situation, and apologizing again.

"No, no, it's all right, but…when you're done there, you need to come here."

"What's wrong?"

"I think, at some point, your killer might have been here…this may be silly, and it may be nothing…"

Something else that might be nothing.

Nothing wasn't working out so well.

Kody continued, "And I have evidence. I mean, seriously, this could be nothing. Just drops of paint, or makeup, but I'm feeling strange about it. Some kind of strange instinct…I think I might know who your killer is."

* * * *

"I…I could be overreacting," Kody told Brodie. "And I really don't know why—I guess what he was wearing reminded me so much of what Brent Myerson wears when he becomes the creature that…It gave me chills. Funny—I should have thought more that someone was ripping off our designs, but it just made me uneasy instead."

Jackson and Detective Angus Hilton were outside—where she believed she had seen blood drops.

Kody and Brodie were in her dressing room.

She was in costume for the night's performance, sitting at her dressing table and just finishing with her hair.

Jackson and Brodie had studied the drops, and he'd told her more about their trip to the nearby pharmacy at Detective Angus Hilton's request—and their discovery of the corpse, the woman who had been in the store.

They didn't know what the drops meant yet, if anything—maybe some poor fellow who had cut himself shaving had come up to read one of the advertising posters for upcoming productions that were on either side of the entrance. Maybe someone just had a cut…easy enough to get a cut to cause that tiny amount of blood.

"No, you always report it when you think something might even be slightly wrong," Brodie assured her, reaching for her opening act hat as she set a last bobby-pin into her hair. "Sometimes in life you take chances. When it comes to anything suspicious—safe is better than sorry."

She glanced over at him quickly, accepting the ladies' straw hat her character wore for Act I. Brodie was always…perfect. Perfect for her, and in her mind, perfect for anyone. She was fairly tall—5'9"—and she loved his solid 6'4". He had the darkest hair she thought she'd ever seen, and eyes as deep and blue as the ocean, along with a handsomely rugged jaw and striking features.

He was also polite and courteous, especially to those who needed help. He was good at laughing, and at honesty…

And he saw the dead, as she did now.

Brodie was, she knew, an amazing investigator and would soon become an amazing addition to Adam Harrison's Krewe of Hunters. But she'd never imagined she'd be doing children's theater so quickly and easily or taking on a leading role in a major show. She'd also never imagined that an investigator accidentally on the job during murders in Key West would wind up being the mainstay of her existence, her best friend, an amazing lover, and basically, her life.

"The woman you found…is there an I.D. on her yet?" she asked. "I feel…well, a little like a kid crying 'wolf.' You and Jackson were on a case…"

"Which started because a woman looked past Halloween and feared someone might be in trouble, or at the least, causing trouble. Kody, trust me. You did the right thing. And with what went on at the pharmacy—a matter of a few blocks from here—it only makes sense for us to have an especially heavy presence here." He came around the dressing table and she turned to look at him.

"It's not just what we think are blood drops that's bothering you, is it?" he asked.

She inhaled and winced. "I think I'm being silly," she murmured. "I mean, Clara saw the guy, and she just appreciated a good performance. While I saw…"

"Hey," he murmured, smoothing a tiny stray hair back from her forehead. "The situation in Key West is not that far in the past."

She nodded. She still missed her friend, a laid-back singer who could be a bit off the wall—but someone she had loved dearly.

It wasn't that long since Kody had nearly been killed.

"I just can't become paranoid!" she said.

"No." He was quiet a minute. "There's no way out of what I do—well, I mean there would be—"

"Never. It's what you do, and you do it well—and you save lives," she told him passionately.

"But we'll be smart—and safe. We'll hang out at the shooting range, so you become a good markswoman—and can handle weapons safely. Too many guns on the streets. And, I'm willing to bet, you're wicked with a can of pepper spray—and you do remember to carry it, right?"

She nodded gravely. "Always." She grinned. "Unless I'm on stage. Well, unless it's a period Brown Bess or a flintlock musket or—"

"I get the idea." He smiled. "And, believe me, the crime scene techs are collecting that blood. Jackson is here, I'm here. We can't do too much until we get an I.D. on our dead vampire girl, or someone else calls in with info or we get to the autopsy tomorrow. I'll be here."

She jumped up and into his arms, careful not to crush her costume too badly. "And here, of course, there are always friends—and you—and your parents."

He laughed softly. "Ah, yes, my folks. They must be busy haunting one of my brothers."

He grinned, holding her tightly for a moment. Looking up into his eyes, she thought again of what strange twists and turns life—and death—could bring. She was so in love with him. She could remember being wary when he had informed her that yes, he saw the dead as well. He had been there for her when so much had gone so wrong.

And he had also taught her to be strong when she'd been terrified.

She was going to be strong now, she determined. He had just found a corpse; she had seen an entertainer in the street. She rose on her toes and kissed him, meaning it to be quick and light, but the kiss deepened, and she felt warmth growing within her...a memory of just how close they had become.

She stepped back quickly. It was opening night and her call was any second.

He smiled, a twisted grin on his face. They had both been thinking the same thing.

It was far too easy to let their minds wander to a place where costumes were stripped away, where there was nothing but the feel of flesh against flesh, of...

"All right, I'm heading out. I'll be in here--somewhere. And Adam is coming in too, I believe—after all, the theater is truly his baby." He winced. "If anything—"

"And if you have to leave, you leave," Kody said determinedly.

He nodded and stepped out of her dressing room.

She watched him go, smiling a little. She was anxious for the show.

And just as anxious to go home.

Dressed and ready, she decided to take her place in the wings. Clara would be ready with all the calls on the tech script, and she'd be near a friend and able to greet other members of the cast.

The basement area was a bevy of activity. She greeted friends who worked in lighting and costumes, sets and props, and stopped to thank Ginny Granger, an attractive woman in her fifties, dark-eyed and whimsical; she liked to keep different streaks of color going through her white hair. Magenta one week, purple the next—and then, maybe green.

There had been a small tear in her cape. Now, like magic, it was gone.

"Ginny, you're the best, and thank you," she told the woman.

"My pleasure—you're the easiest woman I know to dress!" Ginny replied. She wrinkled her nose. "And trust me, I've worked with some whiners in my day." She lowered her voice. "Now that Brent Myerson, playing the good doctor. Ooh, la, la!"

"Brent? He's not...friendly and easy to work with?" Kody asked, surprised. As an actor, Brent was wonderful. He knew his lines. He knew how not to step on someone else's lines. He was great with blocking, with working with others—a true ensemble player.

"Oh, no, I didn't mean that at all. I meant he was just as nice—or nicer—than anyone could imagine. I know you're not doing the next play, but I believe he's got a co-starring role in *The Harvest*. I've just worked with some people who whine about everything. The kind of fabric, the style, or the cut—things the director has chosen to use. Not here so much, just...well, you never know. There are actors, and there are whiners. I like working with actors. I mean, the real Brent Myerson is the nicest man in the world, bar none!"

"The *real* Brent Myerson?" Kody asked.

Ginny was quiet for a minute, glancing around. "He's been great here. I...I mean, everyone deserves a second chance, right? I know he went into treatment. But..."

"Please, Ginny—I'm opening out there with him tonight."

Ginny sighed, glancing around. "He had a drug problem a few years back. He was going to work for one of the summer Shakespeare companies. But like I said, I know he went into treatment. And I'm sure he's fine. He did that soda commercial, and it's a good commercial—he's charming, when he's himself, and I know he wanted treatment. He's worked hard since then. I've seen how great he's been. Please don't say anything."

"No, no, I won't," Kody assured her. She smiled. Brent had been great. In his mid-thirties, he was handsome and charming, and had real gifts. Whether on stage or screen.

The show had been running the entire month of October, and she hadn't seen any sign whatsoever Brent might have gone back on drugs.

Ginny smiled and hurried on, carrying an armful of the winter capes that were worn in Act II.

Kody turned to head toward the stairs and was startled when she was nearly knocked over. She was just as quickly caught and steadied, and found herself staring at a very concerned Percy Ainsworth.

"Sorry, sorry, sorry! We had a faulty bookcase and I'm on my way up. You lean against it in Act II—and if you went through...I wouldn't just feel like a failure, I'd feel terrible!" he told her.

Percy was a slim pile of energy. A man who loved the theater and took incredible pride in his work. He was rather ageless; he shaved his head, so he was bald. His eyes were a bright green that often seemed to shimmer with excitement. And he could manage just about any project quickly and easily, and understood what problems singers and dancers might encounter on stage as well as actors.

"Thanks, and not to worry at all. I'm so glad you're fixing the bookcase. Go, go, hurry!"

He ran ahead of her.

Kody started up the stairs then paused, having the strangest feeling that someone was behind her.

Well, of course, someone was behind her—cast and crew were everywhere.

But there wasn't anyone behind her. A few of the chorus and ensemble members were milling together by a costume rack.

No one was close.

She had a show to do. She had to stop being so ridiculous.

She started up the stairs, and as she did so, she felt a rush of air behind her.

Maybe the beautiful Caroline and her beloved Judson did haunt the theater after all.

She was startled to feel as if someone had been shoved away from her.

"*No! It is not your theater!*" she thought she heard.

A chill—something she had so recently cast off—settled over her.

Turning again, she saw no one.

But she did see the door to one of the set and design studio rooms slide closed. Very softly.

Had someone been behind her?

Had they been speaking to her?

Or was she simply letting her frightening past invade her present?

She hurried on up the stairs. She had a lead in a show—and she was going to do the entire theater, Adam Harrison and all her friends, just as proud as she could.

Chapter 3

The theater was alive with what seemed like an electric energy—just as a theater should be.

The doors had opened at 7:00 P.M. for the night performance.

Some theatergoers mingled in the lobby, box office personnel were taking tickets, and some people were choosing to get to their seats early. Before the seating in the mezzanine and the balcony, there were small bars where snacks and drinks might be purchased. Men and women milled in those areas as well.

Brodie headed to the lobby. In spite of the two blood experts who had arrived from the D.C. forensic unit, there was no difficulty getting the theater crowd in and seated. There was a large open gallery in front, so the techs had been able to rope off an area.

No matter their shirts—identifying them for what they were— people seemed to think they were some kind of a construction crew.

Or just dressed up for Halloween.

"Mr. McFadden!"

He turned. Charly Atwood, box office manager, dapper and ready for tonight's show, walked over to him, a hand extended.

"Great to see you—and congratulations!"

"Thanks, and…on?" Brodie asked.

"Why, Miss McCoy, naturally—you are engaged to a stunning young woman."

"Thanks, yes," Brodie told him.

"It's great," Charly said, beaming. "I can't tell you what an amazing addition Kody has been to the theater—she is the real deal. I saw her sing with her dad on stage years ago, and she was terrific. We're so lucky to have her—all thanks to you. Her show today was sold out—and she segues right into performing."

"She is pretty wonderful," Brodie agreed. "Have you seen Jackson Crow?" he added.

Charly nodded. He'd been informed that a small crime scene crew was coming to check out what had appeared to be blood drops at the theater's entrance.

"I think they're finishing up out there." He lowered his voice because people were milling and chatting in the lobby as they made their way to the ticket-takers. "Heard on the news that Halloween turned real, and a woman was found dead not far from here. So, naturally, you're tracking any possible clues. Such a shame. People having fun…and then someone evil in the middle of it. Sorry, I'm sure you're busy. Jackson is right outside. But if you are trying to see this performance, curtain goes up in ten minutes."

"Thanks, Charly."

"We're a sell-out. I didn't reserve seats. I figured if you or any of the others made it, you'd catch it from the wings. No one asked for a reserved seat—I'm hoping that's fine."

"Absolutely, Charly. No problem," Brodie said, starting past him.

He skirted around the tape that blocked off the area with the blood and headed out. Jackson was speaking with one of the two techs who had come to inspect the drops and take samples. He saw Brodie coming out and spoke quietly to him.

"We'll find out if these are blood—and if they belonged to our vampire-girl," Jackson said. "What are you doing out here? You should be enjoying the show."

"Yeah, I'll go in soon. Curious out here, though. What do you think?"

"I think it's damned odd, and hopefully nothing. But the blood just begins—and ends. Almost as if…"

"As if someone purposely created a little trail—knowing that someone would see it?" Brodie asked.

"Yeah. But—why?"

"Here's the bigger question. The woman in the store saw our corpse—when she was still living. She was bloodied up when she went into the pharmacy. She went out—knowing the police were coming.

So, had she attacked someone—or had someone attacked her before she was killed? Or had her injuries been so bad that she brought herself to a rich man's Halloween cemetery to die?"

"Nothing we can do on that end until the autopsy tomorrow," Jackson said. "But she was bloodied up. I think she'd been attacked."

"Or had she taken the vampire thing too seriously and attacked someone else?" Brodie asked.

"Either way, the entire District, Virginia, and Maryland are on alert—every law enforcement agency in existence has been notified. Not that they're not ready on Halloween from the get-go. Go on in and watch Kody—hey, we had a great line-up of directors/actresses here to begin with, but Kody has brought it all to another level. Go watch her be wonderful."

Brodie nodded and turned to head back toward the stage.

Dealing with violent crime, kidnapping—and murder. It was what they did. Crimes were seldom solved overnight. Blood analysis took time, DNA took time, hunting down leads took time—and often, an army of people working.

Tonight, however, he felt uneasy. The vampire corpse. She hadn't been a vampire. She'd been dressed up in Victorian garb to resemble the common concept of a vampire or part of a vampire's harem, *à la* Bram Stoker.

She'd had blood all over her mouth—and it had seemed she'd been crazy before she'd died.

Close. Far too close to the theater.

As he walked the side aisle to reach the stage-left wing, he noted the audience was indeed full. Most people were in regular clothing, some more dressed up than others. A few sported shirts that said something about Halloween, or outfits resembling those worn by characters in movies, such as Sally in "The Nightmare Before Christmas."

There was still chatter as he walked along, but as he did so, the announcement to please silence cell phones came on and the lights began to blink.

He hurried up the stairs to the wing and silently walked behind the curtain. Clara Avery was standing at the stage manager's podium. She smiled when she saw him take up his silent position. She then nodded toward Kody, who was set for her entrance across the stage. Kody smiled at him and he gave her a thumbs-up sign.

Brent Myerson was standing near Clara, ready to enter for his first monologue. Rory Jenson, as his assistant—known simply as Sasha—was there, too.

The house went dark and the stage lights went up. Brent walked out on stage, striding to his desk, looking at his notes. Rory followed him, and Brent turned, beaming at Rory and starting his opening monologue. Speaking about the wonder of his life, his beautiful fiancée—and the near success he was having with his experiments.

Rory warned the doctor, still into his monologue—his experiments not in creating life but rather saving special lives by borrowing body parts that were sound and...fresh—that his fiancée was on her way.

A fiancée who—like most others—would not like him playing with body parts from the recently deceased.

The good doctor hurriedly put his notes away.

Kody made her appearance on stage. She was welcomed into the arms of the doctor, who spoke about their wedding, and then he went off-stage, and Kody moved into her song.

Brodie understood why the others had thought that Kody would be so perfect for the role. The score had been written in a way that gave it a bit of a rock sound—even in a ballad such as the opening number. Kody's husky alto was perfect for the music.

The song was about dreams, and her character's fears those dreams would not be realized. There was something wrong in her perfect life and her perfect day.

And her perfect man.

She finished the song, standing on stage to the sounds of thunderous applause.

She was great. The audience loved her.

And he got to go home with her.

The first act continued. Kody's character worked on the upcoming wedding, her moving into the doctor's massive castle, and her fears that something just wasn't right. The musical numbers were all brilliant. Her with the doctor. Her asking his assistant, Sasha, what could be wrong—a number that had a great deal of humor to it, perfect before the last number of the first act. That one featured the doctor and Sasha, out in a graveyard, digging up a young man who might have been murdered, but who had the perfect body for experimentation.

Every single performance brought applause from the audience. And as the crowd quieted, intermission was announced.

Brodie decided not to deter Kody in any way—she had a costume change—but to run out and check with Jackson.

Jackson had news for him.

"We might have found out the identity of our corpse, and she's one of the missing persons Angus told us about. She was last seen with friends at the Smithsonian, sketching—she was an artist—and didn't show up when she was supposed to join them for dinner. Her name is Helena Oldham."

"It can't be too easy to kidnap someone out of the Smithsonian."

"No—and there are cameras. I want to stop this quickly. Angus has asked for footage from the museum and we already have two members of a tech crew going through it. We might have something by the time of the show tomorrow. Oh, and Angela ran out of here today because she got a call from a detective in Alexandria. He was contacting the Krewe because he had a missing person's report regarding a young woman, Serena Major, who was kidnapped—by a vampire. He's faxed her the information he has with names and addresses of witnesses."

Brodie was quiet a minute, reflecting on Kody's words earlier—*I know who your killer is.*

There was no way any law enforcement officer could bring in a suspect with nothing—except for a woman's unease because she'd seen something that inexplicably gave her chills.

And no A.D.A. could prosecute anyone on gut instinct.

"Did you see any street performers out here tonight?" he asked Jackson.

Jackson shook his head. "Plenty of kids and adults in costume, but no performers. At least, none of them were performing anything when I saw them. I've been pretty much right here. Why?"

"Kody said someone wearing a mask a lot like the one worn by Brent when he becomes his own monster was dancing out here. I guess a few of the others at the theater saw him too."

"And?" Jackson asked.

He hesitated. "Kody suggested he might be the man who killed our vampire girl."

"Because?"

Brodie shrugged. "Because he gave her chills."

Jackson didn't gainsay him or laugh. He shrugged slightly. "I'll keep my eyes open."

"Great. I need to get back to the show. Maybe we need to start on this tonight."

"Cops and agents are on duty. Go watch your fiancée's last stellar performance for this show."

"Yeah, yeah, right, thanks," Brodie told him. He still wasn't happy as he made his way back to the wing.

* * * *

Everything seemed to be going along as usual.

Live theater, of course, was different every night. Each show was new. New for those in the audience, and new for the actors because of the reactions of the audience.

But…

It seemed normal.

Brent and Rory performed together as the experimentation began.

And as the experimentation went to hell.

The staging for that part was exceptionally well done, in Kody's mind. Brent, as the doctor, staggered and fell, having injected himself with a serum instead of the corpse. He was wired so that little shoots of electricity seemed to jump from his body. He fell—beneath the slab that held the pieces of his corpse, including the brain—from which he had just extracted materials for his serum.

When he fell, a stage hand was there, ready to give him the death's head mask he would wear as he became a monster himself, alive with the brain cells of the man he and Sasha had dug up—a convicted killer.

It was an incredible role, and Brent played it magnificently.

Kody's character entered the laboratory…and found him.

He would threaten her, struggle within himself, profess his love…

And come at her.

Then, a chorus of townspeople summoned by Rory's character would come in and save her; the show ended with a husky ballad about love and loss and life.

Tonight, however, Brent seemed to be all over the place. Mixing up his lines.

Trying to make it through the production, Kody looked at Sasha—in or out of character, his reaction would be the same.

He was puzzled, worried, and even afraid.

She kept moving away from him, trying desperately to create a new blocking that would play to the audience.

And then she remembered what Ginny had said to her.

Drugs.

But Brent had been clean. She'd chatted with him at the start of intermission, before changing for Act II. And he had been fine. What the hell could he have taken that would have caused this kind of change so quickly?

He paused suddenly, center stage, throwing his arms out, as if encompassing the theater.

"Halloween!" he shouted.

It wasn't one of his lines.

And he went on. "If my murder is not solved in the days to come, I will see to it that no more holidays will be celebrated here—ever! Do you hear me? Ever! I died in a pool of blood, and you will find the truth!"

He spun to stare at Kody.

"Or before the next occasion, you too will die in a pool of blood."

Every member of the audience seemed to be sitting on the edge of his or her chair.

For a second, a split second, Kody was frozen.

Stoned! The bastard had done something, and he was stoned!

She didn't want to see him die in a pool of blood—she did want to smack him hard in the face, beneath the mask.

But...

"Sasha!" she cried. "Get help. Get help, for the love of God, Sasha! Your master has gone insane!"

"The people!" Rory told her. "They are just at the gates. They've suspected he defiles the dead. They're ready…"

He ran off stage.

Brent didn't come near her. He stared at her.

Then, as the "townspeople" began to rush on from stage left, Brent sprang across the floor—heading out stage right.

The townspeople floundered when there was no Brent to accost. But they quickly rallied, going into the number that cried for his death before racing after him.

Kody went into the last song, heard the applause, bowed, and waited for the curtain call.

The curtain went up, but Brent did not come on stage. It went down and went up, and Rory rushed out. And then the townspeople, and then...

It went down on the last performance of the play.

And Kody hurried off-stage, rushing over to Clara to demand, "What the hell is going on? I'm going to kill Brent!"

Brodie was there, watching from the wings. He glanced her way, muttering as he strode across the stage in Brent's wake, "I didn't think that was right."

She ran after him. Clara did the same, her features tense, torn between anger and worry.

Extras, stage hands, prop masters, and "townspeople" were all muttering. Angry that one of their number had pulled such a stunt on the last night.

Brodie was ignoring them all, brusquely excusing himself as he made his way down the stairs and to the dressing rooms.

The door to Brent's dressing room was closed. Locked.

Brodie shoved a shoulder against it and the lock gave.

Brent was there, minus the mask.

The stage hand, Barry Adair, who should have helped him with the mask, was there too.

They were both prone on the floor.

"Brent!" Kody said furiously, rushing over to him.

But Brodie stopped her. He dropped down by Brent, checking his throat for a pulse, and then he moved over to Barry Adair and did the same.

His eyes met hers..

"Call 911, quickly. Get emergency services out here. We might just save their lives."

Chapter 4

"We're doing every conceivable test," Dr. Lawrence Butler said. "But…you say that Mr. Myerson was perfectly fine during the first act of the play, then there was a fifteen-minute intermission—and by the end he was…different?"

Brodie looked at Kody. He was in the waiting room at the hospital with her, Clara, and Jackson Crow.

"I spoke with him at the beginning of intermission and he was fine—just fine," Kody said. "But after that, even when I wasn't on stage…he got worse and worse. And he was saying lines that weren't in the play, and then—he raced off stage."

"Naturally, we questioned cast and crew. He ran straight from the stage to his dressing room. The show ended before we went after him and there was a curtain call, so it was at least fifteen minutes between him running off the stage and us finding him," Brodie said.

"What about your young stage hand, Mr. Adair?" the doctor asked.

Clara shook her head. "He wouldn't have seen him. His role is to slip in behind the rear curtain and give Brent the mask during the transformation."

"And we couldn't find anyone who saw him after Act I," Jackson supplied. "It's some kind of a drug overdose, but I can't imagine what acted so quickly—and then knocked them out cold."

"Thank you. Yes, it's hard to treat such things when we don't know what we're dealing with. Is there liquor kept backstage?"

"Not that I know of," Clara said. "People gift performers with all kinds of things, but…Brent didn't drink. At all."

"He'd had a drug problem at one time," Kody said. "But he was in treatment years ago—and, from what I understand, he's been clean since."

"He worked on Broadway last season," Clara said. "Yes, he was clean. I guess"—she turned and looked at Brodie and Jackson—"he slipped? It can happen, I suppose. I mean, of course, we knew. Because Adam Harrison owns the theater, we know about everyone we hire."

"Well, I'm thinking liquid LSD. Was that ever a drug of his choice?" the doctor asked.

They all looked at Clara, who was the one who would know.

She shook her head. "Grass and pills. When he cleaned up, he gave up everything. Absolutely everything. He said he'd been told that even a few drinks could cause him to believe he should be doing drugs. And he didn't want to take a chance. He was dedicated to his recovery and never minded talking about it."

"Well, I do believe both men will pull through. You called in the nick of time. I think we'll discover it was LSD. But something else too, for them to have blacked out so completely. They were almost comatose."

"We'll be looking into the situation," Jackson promised.

The doctor nodded. "And we'll keep you apprised of any changes."

"Doctor, we're going to keep a man here as a precaution," Jackson said.

Brodie looked at Jackson, grateful the head of the Krewe had made that decision.

Something just didn't seem right.

Well, things weren't right. A missing girl had been found— covered in blood before she'd wound up dead in a fabricated cemetery.

Kody had been frightened by a street performer.

Brent had gone crazy on stage—and in that craziness, he had threatened Kody. He had said he'd died in a pool of blood, and if his murder wasn't solved…

"Go home, you two," Jackson said after the doctor moved on. "I have agents coming in—Krewe agents. They'll watch over things here. You've had long days."

Kody was still in her costume. "I should go back—"

"No," Jackson said firmly. "Go home. Clara—you too. Straight home. Adam was at the theater, and we have more of our number making sure everything is closed down safely and securely. "

He glanced at his watch. "Only an hour left of Halloween. Thank God. And Brodie, autopsy on our vampire girl tomorrow, scheduled for nine A.M."

"I'll be there," he promised, slipping an arm around Kody.

She seemed fine; if anything, a little angry. Of course, people at the hospital were looking at her a little strangely—maybe not as strangely as they would have, had it not been Halloween.

"Clara—" Kody began.

"Kody, please, I'm good—"

"I'll get Clara home. Thor was coming to the hospital, but I told him we were all leaving as soon as our night guards arrived. Go, please, get some rest," Jackson said.

"Yes, but—" Kody began.

"The beauty of the Krewe is that we know each other, and we know what's up with what we do. Other agents will take over, Kody."

Brodie nodded over her head to Jackson and led Kody out. It was a short trip from the hospital to their home in Alexandria.

Trick or treaters were off the streets by then.

They passed by only a few adults who had been at parties and were still in costume, either walking from bar to bar or party to party or to their cars to call it quits for the night.

As he drove, though, he knew he was on the lookout for a man in a mask.

A death's head mask.

"Brodie...I worked with Brent Myerson all through rehearsals and through a month of performances. I still don't believe..."

"Kody, it was a long and hard day for everyone. And who can say? Maybe Brent...maybe he felt he just needed a little pick-up and didn't realize what he'd done."

She was silent a minute. "What about Barry?"

"A star like Brent asking him if he wanted a little something? Kody, it's possible."

She shook her head firmly. "Brent...I knew. I knew from the time I saw that performer in the street. Silly, yes. Ridiculous. But...the mask was so similar. A rip-off. I don't know how or why, but—tonight was no accident. I don't believe Brent took anything on purpose."

"You think someone slipped him the drug—liquid LSD or whatever it may prove to be?"

"I do—it would be easy enough. He likes tea. I think someone got in there and slipped something into his tea. And he and Barry were great friends. They might have been talking about the bit of stagecraft they had when the mask was passed to Brent. And Brent would have asked Barry if he'd like some tea, too."

"Kody."

"Yes?"

"It might have just been a slip-up. Hopefully, Brent and Barry will be fine. And—really, thanks to you—the show went off beautifully. The audience didn't even know. Wouldn't know—unless they were return guests. And even then, they might have thought there had been a bit of a rewrite at the end. You were superb."

"Thank you," she said. "But—"

"Kody, seriously, the incidents might have nothing to do with each other. We're on the hunt for a killer, but what happened at the theater might have been…just a slip. It happens. And it doesn't mean Brent won't recover and won't be fine. For now…let's get a good night's rest, huh?"

He wasn't sure at all of what he was saying to her, but he managed to get conviction into his voice.

And yet, as he drove, he kept his eyes open for a man in a death's head mask.

Dancing in the street.

* * * *

They arrived at their small house. There was a gated entry, and a guard on duty at all times.

He or she stood behind bullet-proof glass.

Brodie had also had an excellent alarm system installed, and if they needed more…

Well, he woke at the drop of a pin.

And they had Kody's cat—Godzilla.

He was one humongous cat—and did alert them with very loud

meows if someone was coming to visit.

Their alarm and their living circumstances weren't by accident. Brodie knew he was heading into a dangerous life—not to accept that it could come home on them would be insane. And yet, he didn't want it to be a major part of their lives.

To think their dead vampire girl might come at them in any way was stretching the realm of worry, he told himself.

And it wasn't just the girl. She had been identified. She had disappeared from the Smithsonian, and they knew nothing else yet. She might have run off and joined a cult—a deadly cult. She might have been on so much PCP she'd done the injury to herself.

She might have injured someone else. But as yet, there were no reports from hospitals—or morgues—regarding anyone bleeding to death, or who had bled to death.

It was just...

Halloween.

Thankfully, it would be over in twenty minutes now.

Brodie drove into the garage and hopped out of the car as Kody did the same. She had already moved around to the kitchen entrance to key in the alarm and unlock the door. He followed her.

There were always low lights on in the house. And in the dim kitchen, she turned into his arms, eyes glittering beautifully like a cat's in the night, gold and green and striking. He pulled her against him, remembering the kiss they'd shared earlier—and feeling the bone of the costume corset she was wearing.

"How the hell do you wear that damned thing?" he whispered against her lips.

"Well, I really could do without wearing it now," she murmured in reply.

He laughed, spinning her around—and staring at the tangle of strings at her back. "Wow. I—uh—I should be better than this. It's all knotted...the strings."

"If you just—"

"Hush." He kissed her neck. "If there's a will, there's a way."

He fumbled for a kitchen drawer, drawing her with him. He found scissors and simply cut the woven thread that looped in and out of the corset.

She spun around, staring at him in surprise.

"What? It's just a cord. They can replace it."

"I wasn't thinking it was a bad thing—I'm rather grateful you're thinking on your feet."

He pulled fabric and bone and lacing from her, letting it fall to the floor. She remained in a white cotton slip and period boots, but her breasts and shoulders were bare. And in the low light of the kitchen, she was suddenly unbearably beautiful. She reached up to draw the pins from her hair and it fell around her shoulders like dark gold, curling softly against her bare flesh.

He pulled her back to him in a deep kiss, their tongues playing a sensual dance. His fingers moved over her shoulders and down her back, and he felt her hands on him, lowering down his back to his buttocks.

Then the cat—Godzilla—let out one of his bloodcurdling meows.

They both jumped, then laughed.

Godzilla wasn't worried about an outsider. He was staring up at them, wanting attention himself.

"Later, cat," Brodie promised. He caught Kody's hand and hurried through to the parlor and up the stairs to the master bedroom—where he shut the door.

Godzilla would curl up on the sofa in the parlor—and keep guard.

In the master he twirled Kody around and shook his head slightly before saying admiringly, "You wear that Victorian slip especially well. Magic—you, spinning in the moonlight, hair flying around you."

"Ah, so poetic," she teased, coming to him. He'd set his gun and holster on the dresser, and she slipped his jacket from him. They kissed again as she played with his buckle and zipper, and their mouths barely parted as he made his way out of his shirt, half-tripped on his trousers, and kicked off his shoes.

He still had his socks on when they fell on the bed. She was wearing the slip and undies and her Victorian boots. They laughed, touched and rolled. He looked deeply into her eyes, like fire, beautiful and brilliant, and so expressive. Then his lips traced over the length of her body, intimate and deep, as she whispered his name, arched, writhed and moved against him, and they were together.

It wasn't until the sweet richness of climax seized them both that they eased, gasping, back to reality and cool damp sheets and the night. She laughed softly again. "Wow. You're still in socks, and I'm in boots."

"Sexy, huh?" he grinned.

"I don't know—they say you know you're an old couple when a guy wears socks to bed."

"What about boots?"

She grinned and rolled to an elbow. "Boots? On a woman? Just sexy!" she teased.

"Hm," he said thoughtfully.

"No?" she queried, as if hurt—or as an excuse to grace him with a punch to the arm.

He shook his head, smiling. "You are the sexiest creature in the world—with or without boots."

"Good answer," she told him.

With his peripheral vision, he saw the bedside clock as he drew her back to him.

12:44 A.M. Halloween was over.

Thank God.

He kissed her, and they began to make love again, his energy miraculously and tremendously climbing.

* * * *

There was something about dreaming, or perhaps, the way Kody dreamed.

She *knew* she was dreaming, but that world seemed just as real and solid as the world did during her waking moments.

She was back in Key West. Back at the bar where one of her dearest friends had died—only to return in a most curious way.

She was at the bar, the Drunken Pirate, just outside the Tortuga Shell Hotel, where he had played—and where he had also died. But that was in the past, and as a ghost, he seemed content enough. They sat at one of the tables in the rustic patio area. A new entertainer was playing, the sound pleasant. Near them, palms danced in the breeze, and they could hear the lap of waves out on the ocean. The sun was brilliant, creating dapples of yellow and gold on the water. There was laughter around them. It was a vacation paradise.

"You have to use what you know," he was telling her earnestly. "Use your expertise. That's the most important thing. Never take anything lightly, my dear. Sing like your dad—but remember, history is what you love most. Ah, yes, entertainment!"

Cliff sat back, happy to watch as someone walked up to the stage.

It was Brent—or someone else in Brent's monster costume.

Like the death's head figure who had performed out on the sidewalk.

He repeated the words from the play—*the wrong words Brent Myerson had thrown in that night, high as a kite on whatever!*

"If my murder is not solved in the days to come, I will see to it that no more holidays will be celebrated here—ever! Do you hear me? Ever! I died in a pool of blood, and you will find the truth!"

He began to dance, as he had danced on the sidewalk.

Then he turned, that leering death's head with its black, gaping mouth directed straight at Kody.

He pointed at her.

"Or before the next occasion, you too will die in a pool of blood!"

Chapter 5

Jackson had called bright and early. The agents watching Brent and Barry throughout the night and now into morning were reporting all was quiet. Both men were stable, and by the afternoon, they should be able to talk.

Brodie quickly showered and dressed.

Watching Kody sleep, he told himself they'd both lose their minds if they took every case personally. Yes, there had been blood droplets at the theater. But it could still have been anything.

Kody had been disturbed by a performer in the street. And then on stage, when it came time for him to wear a similar mask, Brent Myerson had come into some kind of hallucination and started ranting that he'd died in a pool of blood. And Kody would do the same.

No connection. They all knew that the theater was supposed to be haunted by the ghosts of Caroline Hartford and Judson Newby. But the two hadn't been murdered—and they hadn't died in pools of blood. As far as he could tell, they weren't haunting the theater. And if he knew his parents—which he did, God knew few men could be quite so *haunted* by their parents when they were deceased—Maeve and Hamish would have befriended the ghosts as well.

So what the hell had Brent been going on about?

Nothing—he'd done liquid LSD mixed with something like Special K, most likely, and been flying like a kite.

Candy-flipping, as users and narcs called it.

A delusion, nothing more.

Sliding back into his jacket, Brodie paused as Kody suddenly flung up—jackknifing from sleep as if she were a Swiss army knife. He moved back to the bed, apologizing.

"Sorry, I didn't mean to wake you," he told her, planting a kiss on her forehead and moving back quickly.

She looked amazingly beautiful in the morning. She was the one in the group who hadn't acted in her previous life, but she certainly had the ability to wake up as if she was starring in a soap opera.

"No, no, not to worry—I just woke up," she told him. "You didn't wake me. And I need to get up—I want to get ready and head to the theater. Alexi is still gone, but after what happened…we'll have to talk. And rehearsals start next Monday for the fall show, so…I need to go in."

"Okay," he told her. "I'll feed mammoth-cat before I go. Call if anything happens. Anything—at all," he told her.

"Of course. You're going with Jackson?"

"Yeah. Autopsy. We need to figure out what went on with the girl we found in the makeshift cemetery. Man, I hope people are taking down decorations today. I think crime scene techs—Feds and locals— are done there. Anyway, seems this thing might be widespread. We know our girl was once a responsible working person, loved by those around her. And there are others missing too. So we'll start with what we can find out about what happened to her. And," he added, "we'll see if those blood drops at the theater had anything to do with anything."

She gave him a brilliant smile but he didn't believe it was real.

"Be careful," he told her.

"Hey, I'm the one being paranoid, remember?" she said. "Come to think of it, maybe your parents will be around today. All this going on—your mom, in particular, is usually on top of such things."

"Remember, I have two brothers they love to haunt, too. And both my parents already saw both plays. Knowing them, they were at some other Halloween performance in the city. Anyway, be careful, just because it's a good thing to always be careful, okay? Any worries, fears, whatever – however silly they may be -- call me."

He started to leave the room when she called him back.

"I'm just in on some decision making today, but…I intend to get into really studying every decade the theater existed."

"Because of Brent's ranting?"

She nodded.

He shook his head. "The supposed theater ghosts—"

"I know. Supposedly, there are ghosts here. Caroline and Judson. But I think we need to look for something else. At least try to find out if someone else was killed."

"It was always a public theater—something would have come down through the ages," Brodie said.

"Then again, maybe not," she told him.

He sat down by her on the bed. "This is a serious problem," he told her softly. "Because Brent Myerson is beloved by all—and you say he's usually a fantastic man as an actor—great to work with. And he's in the next production." He inhaled on a long breath. "But you can't work with an actor who is going to go off at any given moment." He didn't know what seemed so off about everything, but he knew he couldn't stop her from going to the theater—from living.

"He was great—really great," Kody said. She shook her head. "I just find the whole thing hard to believe."

"We'll talk with him today and see what he has to say. The same with Barry. Maybe Barry had it out for Brent for some reason, went to see him backstage—and spiked something Brent was drinking," Brodie suggested unhappily.

Kody shook her head. "They got along fine."

"On the surface. Maybe there's something going on that we don't know about. Anyway, I'm going to join Detective Hilton and Jackson at the autopsy. Then I'll check with you. If you're free, we'll go to the hospital together. The two will be lucid by then—I hope. But hey, get straight to the theater this morning, okay? Be careful about what you're doing. Halloween is over—watch out for masked dancers in the street."

He had meant to speak lightly, but he wasn't feeling that light.

And she knew it.

"As I said," she told him softly, "I'd already planned on tearing into the history of the place." She sighed. "Now I'll be doubling down on those efforts."

He stood. He was too close to her. And her hair was disheveled, her skin sleek and bare.

But the day needed to begin. "Don't go anywhere alone."

"There are hundreds of people using the metro," she assured him.

"Go—get on that poor woman you and Jackson found yesterday. Don't worry about me—I go from a gated community to a public metro system." She shrugged, offering him a wry smile. "Not to worry—Thanksgiving is a month off. I have time to find out what's going on."

That was supposed to assure him. But Brent, in his delusional state, had given them a deadline to find out what had happened. And Thanksgiving was fast approaching.

"Not funny," he assured her.

"Get out of here," she said.

"I'm gone." But at the door, he paused again. "Make sure you set the alarm."

"I will. Promise. Go."

It still took a minute.

"Go!" she commanded.

"Your fault," he told her. "Look at you there. Dark gold cascades over naked shoulders, bedroom eyes, just looking at me with a come-hither sheen in your eyes—"

"This is not a come-hither look—it's a simple 'I'm barely awake and need to get moving' look. Go!" she said, laughing and jumping up to tear into the bathroom, calling to him on her way, "Come to the theater when you're able. I do want to be there to talk to Brent." She halfway closed the bathroom door. "This just wasn't..."

"People do slip. The best of people. And they start over."

She nodded and closed the bathroom door.

Finally, he forced himself down to the garage and into the car.

As always, traffic was heavy, even though the hour was early. Still, he arrived in good time at the D.C. medical examiner's office.

A staff of about eighty worked at the D.C. morgue, but that included assistants, clerical staff, and more. Thankfully, Adam Harrison, Jackson Crow, and members of the Krewe of Hunters and the FBI in general—and the D.C. police—were given priority. Dr. Frank Jeffries, who had come to examine the corpse in the Halloween cemetery, was often requested by members of the Krewe.

He was a strange man, tall and well built, and had been, once upon a time, headed to be a major player in the NFL draft pick. But to everyone's surprise, he'd dropped football and headed to college for his medical degree. His profession was a calling to him. While "we speak for the dead" had become a popular slogan due to many documentaries and shows available to the public, Jeffries was as determined as any law enforcement officer to bring the truth to light.

Some officers and agents might have a problem with him. Some wanted facts and the ability to theorize on a crime themselves.

Brodie hadn't known him that long, but the few instances that had brought him to the morgue as a "consultant" had made him find Jeffries to be dedicated. And Brodie never minded any suggestion that might solve a crime.

When he arrived, Jackson was just donning a paper cover to enter the room where the autopsy would take place.

Brodie quickly donned his own and as he did so, Detective Hilton arrived. "Well, leave it to you two. You found our girl. In a bad way, but…"

"Easy enough on Halloween to hide a corpse in a makeshift graveyard," Jackson noted.

"Sad, so sad," Hilton noted. "I've had people going through security footage from the museum. She was off the grounds before whatever happened to her—happened. Unless she willingly went somewhere, somehow…unless there are vampires running around D.C."

"There are those who practice rituals as if they were vampires," Brodie noted.

Hilton looked at the two of them searchingly. "They, uh, they don't exist, do they? I mean, if they did, you guys would know, right?"

Brodie lowered his head, thinking that he'd let Jackson answer that one. He and Hilton had worked together before. Hilton might be curious about their methods, but not enough to really want to know.

"In my experience, no," Jackson said.

"In my experience," Brodie decided to add, "the truth is that when horrible crimes are committed, there's someone alive and human—with a very sick mind—perpetrating the deeds."

"So we're looking for someone who thinks they're a vampire," Hilton said. "Or maybe convinces his victims he is a vampire, or that he's made them vampires."

He shook his head.

"Let's see what the M.E. has to say," Jackson suggested, indicating the door to the room where their victim lay.

Dr. Jeffries was already there by the body, suited up in his mask and white apron, recorder ready for his findings, and his assistant standing by.

Their victim appeared quite different now that her Victorian attire was gone. The corpse had been bathed.

She looked young and defenseless. Her hair was back, tied off to one side.

That made it possible for them to see the puncture marks on her neck.

"You've got to be kidding," Hilton said. "She was bled to death by a vampire?"

"No. She lost a great deal of blood, yes. But dying from loss of blood? No, I don't think so," Jeffries told them. "I'm just beginning, but I'm going to go out on a limb and say that her heart gave in. Was she pierced in the neck and did she bleed there? Yes—but let's see."

He began his examination. Brodie still winced inwardly when he heard the crack of the ribs as Jeffries went in to study the internal organs.

An autopsy was structured. Still, it wasn't that long before Jeffries weighed the heart and studied it and turned to them.

"We're going to need toxicology reports," he said quietly.

"Her heart did stop?" Jackson asked.

"This young lady, I believe, died of an overdose. Of what, obviously, I need toxicology to say precisely. The crazed way she was behaving might suggest PCP, or something of the like. Or a mixed cocktail."

"She was bitten in the neck by someone or something—but she died of a drug overdose?" Brodie said.

Dr. Jeffries looked from him to Jackson and Detective Hilton. "Yes, and I believe that toxicology will tell us more. But from my findings right now, this young lady was in a weakened condition from lack of blood. She died from cardiac arrest—brought on by a massive overdose of a substance or substances to be discovered."

* * * *

Halloween was being torn down.

Decorations, looking the worse for wear, were coming down from shop displays and walls—busy shopkeepers were clearing out their windows.

Christmas was replacing Halloween—only a few windows were sporting turkeys, pilgrims, or other acknowledgements of the American holiday to come before then.

When Kody arrived at the theater, Charly was in the box office, going through the computer and checking on his sheets for the opening of the show that would run through Thanksgiving. She greeted him with a good morning and he hurriedly came through the door that closed off the box office section to greet her.

"Kody, what happened—are Brent and Barry all right? I can't begin to understand how such a change could take place so quickly!"

"I can't either," she told him. She didn't want to discuss what had happened—she was still too disturbed. "Has anyone come in yet?" she asked him.

"You're the first. I am expecting Adam Harrison, too. He wanted to tell you—and Brent—just how well he thought the last show went. I mean…before. Though he was incredibly proud of you—he said you saved the night. He'll be here this morning."

"Thanks. Okay, I'll be sitting in the mezzanine," she said.

"But—"

"Charly, as we have information, I promise we'll share it."

"It's just that—I suggested Brent for the playhouse here. He loves the theater. And he'd worked so hard on being clean. I mean…"

"Hey, there could be a reason. We'll see," Kody said, walking away. At the moment, she wanted to escape him.

She walked into the theater. The set from last night had already been struck. The next show wasn't due to open until the weekend.

She took a seat in the audience, four rows back from the stage, and tried to picture Brent's strange performance as it had happened. She could see where Barry was to slip in to provide the mask and assistance at his cue, and imagined the laboratory set as it had been.

Barry would have had to have been there.

Barry, or…

Someone else.

But how could Barry have followed his cue in the delusional, nearly comatose state he must have been in for them to have found him soon afterwards unresponsive on Brent's dressing room floor?

"I see your mind at work!"

Kody turned at the question. It hadn't been spoken by anyone currently *working* at the theater; Maeve McFadden was making her spiritual presence known at last.

Kody smiled. Maeve must have been amazing in life, drawing attention with her unbridled energy and enthusiasm any time she entered a room. She'd been a beautiful woman, tall and slim, with stunning and refined facial features and brilliant eyes.

Naturally, Hamish was right behind her. They had taken seats in the row right behind Kody.

"I heard you were absolutely amazing, saving the show," Hamish told her.

He was an older version of his sons, dignified gray entering his dark hair. In life, he'd segued from being a heartthrob of stage and screen into a magnificent character actor. Kody often wished she'd met them in life—then again, it was a bit disconcerting that her almost-in-laws were so present in her life, even though they were dead.

"I'm perplexed," Maeve said.

"I knew we should have been here last night, my love," Hamish said to his wife. "Halloween—always a rough time. People...well, people should have the opportunity to dress up and have fun. But as we know too well, there's always an element out there to make ill use of the pleasure others might take during what should be an enjoyable occasion."

"Darling, you wanted to see the concert at the park as much as I did," Maeve protested.

"Of course, of course. But we weren't here. And you have no idea of what happened, Kody? By appearances, Brent had a terrible slip, looped Barry into it, and threatened you on stage?" Hamish asked.

"He was very dramatic," Kody said.

Maeve shook her head. "Overacting!"

Hamish remained serious. "We worked with Brent, years ago—he was a child actor in a dreadful movie we did."

"Dreadful? It was a tremendous box-office success!" Maeve said.

Hamish winked at Kody and shook his head. "Terrible slasher flick. But that's not the point. We should have been here."

"We'd have probably been in the audience anyway," Maeve said. "Enjoying the show—and not watching what was going on. Where was Clara—she was stage-managing, right?"

"And she was right where she was supposed to be—at her podium in the wings, calling action, lights, props…doing her job," Kody said.

"Yes, of course," Maeve said. "But from here on out—we'll be here. And I intend to ask all of you—and dear Adam, naturally—that you not crucify Brent until we know the truth."

"I'm wondering myself. But—who would want to do such a thing? A disgruntled actor, someone who wasn't cast in a show…who would want to do their best to ruin a production?" Kody asked. "Here, I would think it would be difficult to sneak around. Anyone who knows anything about theater in this region would know Adam owns the theater—and he's titular head of a renowned unit of the FBI."

"Who indeed?" Hamish said thoughtfully.

Kody winced, and they looked at one another without speaking.

Because they all knew the answer to that.

Someone within. The threat—if there was one, if Brent and Barry had been duped—had to have come from within. From someone working at the theater in some capacity—someone who could walk by the management, actors, actresses and FBI agents without even being noticed.

Chapter 6

Brent Myerson—customarily a handsome, pleasant, and confident leading man—looked like bloody hell.

He was cognizant—completely cognizant. But he had been crying. His features were taut, pale, and almost ghastly.

Yes, the man was an actor.

Still, Brodie couldn't help but believe every word that came out of his mouth.

"I didn't! I swear I didn't use!" he said, sinking back on his hospital bed and staring up at the ceiling.

He looked like a man declaring his innocence desperately as he stood in front of a firing line.

Maybe this was something like that.

After all, Adam Harrison had come to the hospital along with Jackson, Brodie, Clara and Kody—and his future, if not his life, lay on the line.

He had already professed his gratitude that he had a life to worry about.

Kody, by the bed, squeezed his hand, and Brodie knew she believed him too. Then again, looking at Adam and Clara, he believed they were convinced as well.

"Kody," Brent said desperately. "You saw me at intermission—you saw me, we talked, and I remember every moment of it...I remember Barry coming to my dressing room and telling me the little chink in the mask had been repaired and then...nothing. Nothing—until I came here, and the doctors and nurses were talking to me about the overdose and…oh, God. I didn't. I didn't have anything, I would never lure Barry, I…God, you have to believe me!"

"Who did you see and talk to besides Kody and Barry?" Adam asked.

"Clara—I said I'd be back in the wings, pronto," Brent said.

Clara nodded her agreement—that had happened.

"I passed half the theater!" Brent said. "The prop and set guys changing over to the laboratory. Chorus members down in the basement—our townspeople. I…"

"What about in your dressing room?" Brodie asked. "Did anyone come see you there?"

"Barry. And him coming is…it's the last I remember. I mean, I get snatches. I see someone running around like a lunatic, talking about dying in a pool of blood. And then I see that it's me! But there's something, a voice in my head, saying the lines. I'm insane. That's it. I've gone insane."

"No one besides Barry came to the room," Kody said, still holding his hand, her eyes filled with concern. "So, did you drink or eat anything?"

"My tea, of course. I always have tea in my dressing room between acts."

"Who brings you the tea?" Adam asked him.

"Ginny. She's an absolute doll about it. She's busy with costuming changes between acts, but she makes sure it's in my room. A pot of herbal tea." He winced. "When I gave up drugs, I embraced tea. It was my new thing. I'd go to tea tastings, have something like a 'tea cellar' at my house now. Ginny brings it in about fifteen minutes before the intermission, and it brews. It's perfect for a few quick cups between acts. I use honey and lemon—it helps keep the voice clear."

"Ginny was in the wings with costuming during the intermission," Clara murmured.

"Yes, she helped me," Kody said.

They were all silent for a minute, and then Brent spoke passionately again. "I didn't—I swear—I didn't take anything on purpose. Someone did this to me—someone who wanted to discredit me. I don't know why—I didn't think that I had any enemies." He stared at Clara suddenly. "I know…I know, maybe that Gerrit Lambeth guy—he wanted the role. And he tried out for the pilgrim play we're doing for the next show—he wanted my role in that, too."

"Someone would have seen him, Brent," Clara said.

"I don't know! I swear—I didn't do this to myself. I wouldn't. I was working—happy. I had a problem, yes, still have a problem, but I fight it. I fight the good fight!" Brent swore. "Maybe…maybe—I don't know. There were so many people dressed up."

Brodie glanced over to where Kody was sitting by the bed, still holding Brent's hand. She would have been sympathetic to anyone, but she knew Brent. She'd worked with him. She'd talked about him being a wonderful co-player, that he'd helped her in many ways. She was such a newbie to what they were having her do.

But he believed the man, too.

Brent looked straight at Adam. "I swear on my life, I had no idea I was consuming drugs. I do remember feeling good, but…the play had a great run. I was proud of it. Happy—it was natural to feel good. Trying to feel good is why people take drugs, but I didn't need to—everything was great. Please, please, don't fire me. Please."

"We'll keep investigating," Brodie promised.

"Are you accusing Ginny of having done this thing?" Adam asked.

Brent shook his head helplessly. "Ginny wouldn't hurt me. She wouldn't hurt anyone," he said. "She did me a favor, setting my tea to brew every night. We're not the…not diva oriented. She has done it since we opened, just because she's so nice. And because the little green room has a water heater. She said she was happy I was on tea. That I was a super actor and nice guy, and she'd help me in any way she could. Talk to her—I know she didn't do it!"

Yes, they would talk to her. But if the woman had done it, it wasn't something she was going to admit. Still, they didn't need any search warrants—Adam owned the building. No one leased anything. It was his property and he had the right to do with it as he would.

"We'll check into every possible circumstance," he promised Brent.

Brent nodded miserably. "They're letting me out in a few days. Suggesting rehab, but the show opens. I swear I will not ruin another show." He winced. "How bad was it? Have I become a liability—will no one come if I'm in a show?"

The misery in his voice was deep.

"It was fine," Kody quickly assured him.

"Kody pulled it out of the fire," Clara told him.

Brent looked at Kody with something like adoration. Brodie allowed himself a moment of amusement; he'd be jealous as hell if he didn't know Brent's partner.

"How is Nick, by the way?" he asked. "How is he...taking this?"

"Nick is the best," Brent said. "He believes me. He believes in me." He looked at Adam. "Am I—fired?"

"I let my theater managers do the hiring and firing," Adam said. "But my suggestion is no—for the time being."

Fresh tears ran down Brent's face. The others started to leave. Kody paused to kiss him on the cheek, and then she followed them across the hall to Barry's room.

Results were the same—except Barry wasn't tearful; he was angry. "Was it supposed to be a joke?" he demanded. "Or, worse—were we supposed to die? Doc told me if they hadn't started stomach-pumping and counteracting the drugs when they did...it could have been bad. As in—all over for us bad."

"Tell us who was around from your viewpoint," Brodie suggested.

Barry stared at Jackson, which made sense. Jackson was head of an FBI unit. At the moment, Brodie wasn't officially authorized to make any kind of arrest. Adam was always low key—in the background. He might not have even known Adam was titular head of the Krewe.

"I sure as hell didn't do it! I don't even smoke weed, legal or no. Ask anyone."

"So who did? Do you think Brent did this?" Jackson asked him.

Barry shrugged. "I don't...I don't know. I really like the guy. He's down to earth, you know? Humble. I've worked with a few who think they've been assigned indentured servants."

"Were you with him when he went to his dressing room?" Brodie asked him.

"Yeah, we met in the hall. I was super glad to tell him a mask piece had been fixed. It had been cutting into him. Nothing the audience would notice, but something that must've bugged him. He was never a complainer."

"Did you drink tea?" Jackson asked.

"Sure."

"Did you see anyone do anything to the tea?" Brodie asked.

"No—the tea was there. Some kind of green tea with a hibiscus twist, or something like that. It didn't taste like tea to me to begin with, but I like normal tea, you know?"

"Black tea," Kody murmured.

"Yeah—the normal stuff. If it had been normal tea, I might have tasted something odd."

"You're both pretty sure it was the tea?" Clara asked quietly.

"What the hell else?" Barry asked. "I drank the tea. The walls started moving. Brent looked like a giant ape. Things in the room started dancing. Then I was out. I think I knew before I passed out that I'd been drugged, but…no," he said, staring around at the group of them. "No, I never saw Brent put anything in the teapot. Whatever it was—it was in the room before we got there."

They thanked Barry and left, pausing in the hall to talk.

"It looks like we had someone in the theater—one of our own or someone who slipped in somehow—do this on purpose," Adam said. "You two will take appropriate measures?" he asked. "I try to leave the theater to theater people. Marnie…Clara and Alexi. And now Kody. But whatever happened…we have to step in," he said, glancing at Clara and Kody.

"Of course," they agreed.

"What about the threat?" Clara asked.

Jackson quickly answered, "Brent was stoned out of his gourd. He said whatever came to his mind, but…"

"But," Brodie continued. "They might have been words planted in his head."

"We'll get a thorough search going of the theater—see if we can find drugs or equipment or anything that might indicate how the tea was spiked," Jackson said. "Clara—take a break. Kody—"

"I'm going to start hitting the libraries. Library of Congress, Smithsonian, you name it," Kody told him. "I'm going to know every bit of history that has to do with the theater."

Adam shook his head. "I wanted more research anyway. But Kody…if you're worried about what was said on stage, I can send you both on vacation."

"No," Kody protested. "I'm not afraid—I want to know. I won't be alone in any dark alleys."

"You won't be alone in the theater," he said firmly.

Kody grinned at that. "I take it you're going to do a thorough search. That means lots of cops and tech people. I'm good for a while."

"I'll hang with her," Clara promised. "We'll be careful."

"All right. Keep your phones handy—and Angela will have everyone on alert so that we have Krewe everywhere. Speed dial," he said, shaking a finger at them.

"Speed dial!" they promised in unison.

"All right then," Adam said. "We'll head out."

Brodie looked at Jackson; they'd be headed to the theater. The search would begin now—before anyone else came in. They were lucky -- one season had ended.

The next had yet to begin.

But then again, assuming that Brent was telling the truth, whoever had drugged his tea had already had plenty of time to pick up his—or her—pieces.

And if it was someone connected to the theater...

It was going to be damned hard to prove.

* * * *

Kody looked up from the pile of books in front of her. "It says that ancient Celtic people celebrated Samhain—lit bonfires, wore costumes—all kinds of things," she told Clara, who was sitting across from her at one of the long tables in the library. "In 609 AD, Pope Gregory III designated November 1st as All Saints Day. By then, Britain was turning to Christianity, and many of the Celtic traditions, therefore, were interwoven with the new beliefs. All Saints Day was preceded by All Saints' Eve or All Hallows' Eve, or Halloween.

"In America, at first, it was low—low—key. The Puritans weren't into that kind of celebrating. But bit by bit, other European influences began. And in 1849, the Irish potato famine brought thousands upon thousands of Irish flooding in, and they had their Jack, who in Ireland ran around with a lit turnip to ward off the darkness. Here, the turnip became a pumpkin, and the jack-o-lantern became big." She turned the book so that Clara could see the illustrations.

"Continuing onward, in the 1800s," she went on, "the holiday was religious and also community oriented. People would have dinners, get togethers, perhaps wear costumes. Through the end of the 1900s and into the last century, our leaders tried to tamp down on the witchcraft association—the old Celtic religions being pretty twisted by some—and make Halloween a holiday without mischief, pranks, or the like. There was a population boom in the forties and fifties—baby-boomers—and in that generation, trick-or-treating really took off. After that, adults began having parties. And then card companies stepped into it, and voilà! Major holiday."

"And this year, thank the Lord, it's over!" Clara said and shook her head. "Halloween should be a great holiday. I mean, seriously. For one, to think of those we've lost, but in general for fun. Kids get to dress up. They have a night where candy is okay. And even for adults—It should be fun. But here's the thing—truly sadly, people use the holiday to twist and turn what should be fun into something evil. The Krewe has seen it a few times. At least…"

"At least?" Kody asked.

Clara let out a breath. "At least no one was really hurt at the theater. I mean, Brent and Barry are both going to be okay."

"But if we hadn't gone running to Brent's dressing room, they could have died." Kody paused. "The thing is—anyone around the theater would know his performance would cause some real anger among his fellows. So I don't think either was intended to die. In fact, I think Barry was drugged by accident. He just *happened* to be in Brent's dressing room."

"You could be right."

"Or wrong," she sighed. "Maybe he needed to be out of the picture, so that whoever did the drugging could be the one to get the mask to Brent while he was on stage. And Halloween was the perfect holiday during which to make it happen."

Clara looked at her thoughtfully. "So, Halloween. Do you think…that someone wanted Brent to threaten you with his lines—as he did? Seriously, he was out of it—maybe someone just wanted to throw a wrench in the works."

"That's possible. But I can't help but remember the dancer in the mask so much like Brent's death's head mask. And…"

"And?"

"A girl died. Helena Oldham. They found her in the Halloween cemetery at the mansion. And she died of a drug overdose."

Clara nodded. "It's a whole bunch of maybes, but we have to go with all the maybes. So—"

"Thanksgiving," Kody said. "I know that most kids in America are taught in school that the first Thanksgiving was celebrated by the Pilgrim settlers and the Wampanoag Indians in 1621. People around the country—as it grew—celebrated a feast day, but on different days until 1863, when in the middle of the Civil War, President Lincoln designated a day in November each year as Thanksgiving Day." She inhaled thoughtfully, frowning. "We don't dress up on Thanksgiving. We don't celebrate it with skeleton decorations or anything like that. But it is our next holiday."

"No one dies in the Thanksgiving show," Clara pointed out. "And," she added, smiling, "you're not in it."

"No. But I still think it means something. I've got the book on the theater from the beginning—it was designed by Arthur Rutledge, an Englishman, but a naturalized citizen. He had built a few theaters in England—in Liverpool and in Yorkshire. He was also a theater lover, according to what I have here. The building of the structure took place in 1842. The first show was the 'The Scarlet Letter' and it went up at the grand opening in October of that year."

"You stick with the 1800s and I'll start with the 1900s, seeing what could possibly have happened at the theater. Someone dying in a pool of blood," Clara murmured.

The two of them went back to work.

The task wasn't difficult for Kody. She loved delving into the past—and into the lives of the people who lived in different times, and the social mores that dictated their lives.

She read everything she could on Caroline and Judson. He'd been born to wealth in NYC, but he'd signed up for war, and had proven his gallantry and courage on the field. He was admired and loved—and expected to marry the daughter of someone high in society. He'd fallen in love with Caroline when she had been performing in Shakespeare's "Romeo and Juliet." She had doubted him at first, but when the stage where she'd been working went down, he had purchased the theater for her. He'd loved her so much that his heart had stopped when he'd found her at the foot of the stairs.

No pools of blood. A sad accident had done them in.

Or had it?

Appearances could be deceptive.

This time...

It had been made to look as if Brent Myerson had fallen off the wagon, delved back into drugs. He might well have died, and no one would have thought any differently than he had given way and dragged Barry down with him.

But...if there was something off with the truth about Caroline and Judson...

What had it been?

Who could have caused something to happen, why and...

If so, how the hell had they covered it up?

Chapter 7

"Don't you think it would be just fabulous?" Maeve McFadden demanded. "The theater! What elegant staging, what lighting could be achieved—plenty of seating, of course, and...oh, good heavens, maybe your brothers will even get it together by then. A triple wedding—in the theater! So elegant, with music...Oh, there's an orchestra pit, the music could be so wonderful. Dramatic, yes?"

"*Melodramatic*, Mom...please, come on!" Brodie McFadden protested. "We're getting married—not staging an epic. And—"

"Ah, my dear boy," Hamish McFadden said, indicating Maeve—his wife and Brodie's mother—and continuing with, "marry an actress, dear son, and life is an epic!" Hamish grinned and mused on his own words for a moment. "Life—and death," he added softly.

"Mom, it's not time to talk about the wedding, anyway. Please, we know there is something going on here. If we believe him, someone deliberately tried to either kill Brent Myerson or get him addicted again. Or at the least, ruin the theater. We have a serious situation—"

"You're always going to have a serious situation, son. You've chosen to be FBI, and Krewe of Hunters," Hamish reminded him gently.

"But this situation is *here.*"

They were in the audience area of the theater. While heading to the stage and down to the basement below, Brodie had discovered that Maeve and Hamish were there, in the audience, pointing at the stage.

They knew what had happened. And he knew they had spoken with Kody.

He'd hoped maybe they did know something more—perhaps about a crew member or actor they hadn't remembered.

They didn't. They might have been discussing the situation before he had arrived, but now they had nothing new to add.

Maeve had focused on their personal lives.

"Mom. We will get married. We will plan it. But what I needed to ask you about—"

"We weren't here," Hamish said. "I thought you knew that. I am so sorry."

"And if we had been," Maeve said, "we'd have been watching the show. Proud of our almost daughter-in-law, a lovely young lady who does have the good sense to love the theater."

"I love the theater too—watching it," Brodie said.

"He's a law enforcer. He helps people. We need to be very proud of him—and his brothers," Hamish reminded Maeve.

"Of course," Maeve said. But she was still disappointed. Three sons—and all of them were going into the FBI.

Not an actor among them.

Brodie shook his head, lowering it slightly. He loved his parents, always had and always would—whether they stayed with him and his brothers long in the sense of "in the spirit," or if they eventually felt that they were done with the mortal world and moved on.

They had both been actors themselves—icons of stage and screen. They had perished together in an accident when rigging had failed in the middle of a play.

Died together dramatically—maybe fitting. In death, Maeve was, ironically, still larger than life.

"He is marrying an actress!" Maeve reminded her husband.

"Technically, Bryan is marrying an actress. Kody just opened her own museum down in Key West, and research and history are what she loves," Brodie said. "Right now—"

"She was incredible in that play, and her children's production was outstanding. She is an actress at heart—she just didn't know it. Oh, and her father was a rock star! If you were to marry right in the theater…I know she would love the drama," Maeve said.

All parents wanted to be involved in their children's weddings. His parents—though dead—were no exception.

"Mother—as far as the theater goes, right now? I have to find out the truth of what is going on—and if someone here is involved with the tragic overdose death of a young woman. Okay? I was hoping to catch you two…hoping you might know something. But you don't—"

"We'll be watching now," Hamish vowed passionately.

"Thank you—now I need to start working with the cast and crew around here," Brodie said. He started to walk away, and then paused, walking back to his mother. "Mom, we want a small wedding. Kody had enough with real-life drama back in Key West—and as you pointed out, our lives might always be drama. We're thinking family, a few close friends—and a honeymoon trip somewhere far, far away. And we were actually thinking something staid and traditional—like a church. But please—let's get through this first, okay?"

"Of course, darling, of course!" Maeve said. "Just as long as you marry the girl—soon."

"Yes, ma'am. And we'll keep you apprised all the way."

That settled, he left them, hurried to the stage, and went down the stairs to the basement.

It was crawling with officers and tech personnel. Brodie found Jackson, who looked at him a bit hopefully. He shook his head.

His parents had nothing.

"Ginny is waiting to talk to you in Brent's dressing room. I thought that would be a good area for you two and thought it was better for you to do the talking—since Kody was in the play and worked with Brent."

"Does she think we're accusing her?" Brodie asked.

"Everyone here seems to be a wreck. I've started with the stagecraft personnel and then I'll get to the townspeople. See what Ginny can tell you."

"Okay." He paused, turning back to Jackson. "Have you spoken with Charly Atwood? I'm thinking about the street performer—with the mask like that one used in the show? I don't know why, but he disturbed Kody. Maybe Charly saw something."

"I'll send him back to you," Jackson said.

Brodie nodded and started through the back.

As he made his way to Brent's dressing room, Brodie noted that even here, backstage, the theater was really beautiful. He knew the basics—she was a grand old dame that Adam Harrison had purchased, and once he owned it, he had first hired a crew of electricians and plumbers and structural engineers to ensure that the theater was sound and safe for both the players and the audience. Buying and supporting the theater had been part of the many philanthropic works with which he became involved.

It had proven to be damned good, since several of his agents had wound up partnering with or marrying performers. He hadn't, however, he had to admit, known that Kody would become so involved.

Did this have something to do with her personally? She had been disturbed by the performer in the street. And she had been the one to receive the line about dying in a pool of blood.

He shook his head. No—there would be no reason. Kody was from Florida—she had only been involved with the theater in the last month or so.

He thought that, in a way, all the members of the Krewe of Hunters were performers themselves—always pretending to the rest of the world they did not seek and often receive assistance from the dead in solving cases.

He reached the dressing room. The door was ajar; he went in and found Ginny Granger seated at the dressing table, staring down at her hands.

Today, Ginny had streaks of mauve and orange in her hair, a few shoots of pink, and one streak of emerald green. She looked up at Brodie, misery in her eyes.

"I would never hurt Brent," she vowed. "Never. In a thousand years. He's a good man. A talented man. He gives to every bum on the street. He's polite and courteous to everyone, and that isn't every actor who has worked on Broadway, trust me. I would never hurt him."

"Okay, Ginny. Please, what I'm trying to figure out is what might have happened. I understand you delivered the tea, but you weren't here when Brent came in at intermission. So, tell me everything, from when you brewed the tea until when you left it here."

Ginny nodded, brushing away a silent tear. "I brew the tea in the green room," she said. "Adam Harrison had that set up beautifully— you know, most theaters don't even have one. They're more for television studios and the like. But Adam is always thoughtful. The green room has a refrigerator and a microwave—and a pod coffee machine and a little thing that boils water. I use the little water-boiler.

We have a teapot, naturally, and we have an assortment of teas—tea became Brent's thing. I selected the tea he said he wanted and put it in the little strainer in the pot. I boiled water and poured it in. I put a couple of cups on the tray—I always do. When it was set, I put the tray in his room, and then…"

She broke off, frowning.

"What, Ginny?"

"I left…I hurried out to the rack where the costumes were."

"Why were you frowning? What were you thinking?"

"I saw someone."

"Who?"

"I don't know, but…I remember. I saw someone…something…out of the corner of my eye. I figured it was just Barry heading in ahead of the intermission…with the mask."

"I believe Barry did go in with the mask."

"Yes, I remember, it had been fixed. But I thought later—I mean, I saw him go back again when Brent was in the dressing room."

She appeared to be perplexed, not certain of what she had seen. "I didn't even think about it. I mean, when the show ended, it was chaos, and no one knew…well, Brent denied he just fell back into taking drugs, and I believe him."

"Thank you, Ginny," he said quietly.

There was a tap at the door. Timing couldn't have been better if it had been staged.

"I…don't know what to do. I can't really work on anything—the cops or whoever they are have the place rather torn apart. I'd been going to spend the day working on the Puritan show…"

"Go home. Go to a museum. Go have fun doing something or just getting some rest," he suggested.

She smiled and walked toward the door just as it opened. Charly Atwood was there. He nodded somberly to Ginny.

She hurried on out as Charly came in. He didn't sit.

"Special Agent Crow said that you wanted to talk to me—something about a street performer," Charly said.

The door closed behind Ginny.

"Did she do it?" he asked softly and anxiously. "I'm guessing that you think that someone else drugged Brent, and that it had to be someone behind the stage."

"We don't know what to think yet, Charly," Brodie said. "But I am curious about someone who was apparently wearing a mask similar to the one Brent used. Clara and Kody saw him—or her. I was hoping maybe you'd seen him. Maybe knew who he was—or knew if anyone had come in or out, perhaps managed to slip backstage, after the performance started."

"I am strict," Charly said. "My ushers all know—ticket, ticket, ticket. Unless it's a well-known Krewe member. Or consultant, such as yourself." His eyes widened. "You don't think you have a rogue agent, do you? Or associate. I know Jackson was here, you were here...Clara, stage managing. Angela was here earlier. Most of the Krewe—even those who had hoped to attend—were out of town or engaged. Halloween. It always draws out the crazies."

"So, to your knowledge, no one other than someone with the Krewe—or working the show—could have gotten backstage?"

He winced. "We don't have cops in the wings, but...someone would have noticed, don't you think? And what fool would be crazy enough to sneak into a theater associated with an elite unit of the FBI?" He paused, shaking his head. "But then again, everyone loves Brent, so I can't imagine how anyone working with him would have done such a horrible thing."

"Did you see the street performer, Charly?"

"No, I'm really sorry—I didn't."

"And nothing struck you as unusual about the audience last night?"

"It was Halloween. Everything was unusual," Charly said.

Brodie nodded. "Yeah," he said. "Well, thanks."

As he spoke, there was another knock at the door. This time Charly left as Percy Ainsworth, set designer and head of the stagecraft department, stuck his head in.

"Hey, Brodie, I may have something for you," he said.

Charly waited, as if he needed to hear what was said as well.

"Thanks, Charly. Percy, come on in." He made it clear that Charly was to leave, knowing that he and Percy were friends so they would probably talk later.

But right now, he wanted to hear what Percy had to say—without Charly present.

Charly nodded and left. Percy came in and closed the door.

"I didn't think of this until…until now. I wasn't paying that much attention to people coming and going from the stage. But Ginny mentioned to me someone went into Brent's room—this room—*before* the break. With the mask."

"And?"

"Well, I saw Barry later with the mask, and he was saying he was going to show Brent how it had been repaired. I can't imagine why he would say that if he'd already brought the mask back here. And it got me thinking…there had been a street performer outside with a similar mask. I don't know how the hell he would have managed it, but…I don't know. Maybe someone with a grudge came in off the street, holding the mask up…and anyone working here would have thought whoever it was belonged. I mean, I'm no detective, but hey, that's kind of a no-brainer."

"Did you see anyone at any time?" Brodie asked him.

"Just Barry—right at the intermission."

"Thank you," Brodie said. "If you think of anything else—it doesn't take an investigator to be observant, so…thanks."

"Sure." Percy grimaced. "I'll be hanging around all day, trying to put things back when the cops finish tearing the place apart."

"Okay. I guess there will be a bit of a mess."

Percy headed on out and Brodie followed him. He'd find Jackson and start talking—or listening—with him to the actors who had been "townspeople" in the chorus.

He hesitated outside the dressing room. The theater had a "stage" door, but only because of fire regulations. Thanks to the levels of the ground and the way the theater had been built, it was a stage door that was never used. It was a fire exit at the end of a small hall and almost directly across from the steps that led down to the dressing rooms and prop and set rooms in the basement.

It couldn't be opened from the outside.

The only way in would be if someone opened it from the inside—and then an alarm would go off.

He walked the short distance to the door that was marked "Emergency Exit Only."

He was staring at it when Jackson found him there.

"What?" Jackson asked.

"Charly Atwood swears he didn't see anything unusual—other

than Halloween craziness—last night. And he said his ushers know that no one gets in without a ticket. Unless it's one of us."

"We'll get the forensic team to dust," Jackson told him. "There's an alarm—if this door opens, there's an alarm."

"I know. Still, it's worth checking out. Whatever happened, happened from within here."

"Anything else?"

"Yes. Someone—both Ginny and Percy Ainsworth thought it was Barry—went to Brent's dressing room *before* the intermission."

"Our person from within here," he said. "But we need to leave this to the forensic team now. We have someone else to interview."

"Oh?"

"I've gotten a call from a museum employee. She saw our victim—our dead vampire woman, Helena Oldham, leave the museum."

"We knew she'd left it."

"Yes, but this woman—Vickie Bostwick—was leaving, too."

"Don't tell me…there was a street performer in a death's head mask outside, and Helena stopped to watch him?"

Jackson shook his head. "You're partially wrong."

"There was a street performer out there—wearing some other kind of a mask?"

"You got it. Only, this time, our man—or woman—was dressed up as something else."

"What this time?"

"President Abraham Lincoln."

"The man some consider to be our greatest American President-- and the one President assassinated in a theater," Brodie said.

"The one and only."

"Let's get over there—asap."

Chapter 8

Kody gave her attention to the construction and beginning of the theater.

That was in 1842.

Nineteen years before the first shots of the Civil War had been fired. Arthur Rutledge had managed and maintained the theater himself for five years before he passed away.

She searched out his death records. By every account she found, Arthur Rutledge had died at home, in his bed, of natural causes at the age of seventy-seven.

No pool of blood.

After his death, the theater had fallen vacant for several years. Then it had been purchased by Timothy Bainbridge, a man who had appeared from nowhere, and was suspected to have made his money through ill-gotten gains—he had been a later-day pirate, or so many claimed.

A sea captain, by his own declaration. But apparently, he tended to be where other ships went down, where crews disappeared without a trace, and where other evil things occurred. Nothing could be proven against him, and he was never prosecuted.

"This could be something," Kody said aloud.

Clara looked over at her.

"In 1859, Captain Timothy Bainbridge had 'business' with one of his ships. His journey coincided with the disappearance of the *Kiley Marie*, a merchant vessel. Bainbridge was gone for a year—and he wasn't paying his debts. He seemed to disappear. Rumor went around—supposedly started by one of his men—that he had been injured. So the theater was considered abandoned. And that's when Judson Newby bought it, and he and Caroline—died. Clara, what if Bainbridge was nursing his wounds somewhere, but he got better. And he came back—bitter and vengeful? What if Caroline and Judson didn't die so peacefully, as those who discovered them believed? What if Bainbridge came back and murdered them?"

"Where was your pool of blood?" Clara asked.

"I haven't found a pool of blood yet," Kody said. "But okay, suppose he hid out at the theater, hating the two for taking it over. What if he killed them, and…"

"Someone knew—and killed him?"

Kody nodded. "In a pool of blood—one they managed to get picked up before anyone else ever discovered it? They weren't lighting up crime scenes with luminol back then."

"It's possible—anything is possible. We're talking about events well over a hundred and fifty years ago."

"Okay, how would we ever prove that? Especially since it was so, so long ago, and you've got a dozen books in front of you and can't find more information. If he had been assumed 'disappeared' or 'lost at sea,' there won't be any records on him. And a vengeful ghost—if the man did turn into a vengeful ghost—wouldn't be capable of mixing up the cocktail that downed Brent and Barry."

"No—but any member of the Krewe will tell you that a human being is always involved. The past may influence the present, but there's a flesh and blood killer out there."

"Piracy—as in our old concept of Blackbeard piracy—began to die out in the 1820s. But Bainbridge was supposed to have assailed ships at sea much later, almost into the 1860s. He was never caught, but it seems that most historians credit him with the loss of many ships from different nations. He kidnapped a few 'wives' and had—according to this researcher—about a dozen illegitimate children. He seldom supported them—or their mothers—and there must have been resentment on that. But the wives were all over the place—Florida, Texas, Mexico, and New England." She looked up at Clara, tapping the book she was reading. "The first printing on this book was 1880. And the author tracked down police reports on Bainbridge. He was last seen going to the theater—to the theater! Clara, I think he was killed there. Stabbed or shot—and that whoever is doing this knew about Bainbridge."

"Possibly. When did he disappear?" Clara asked.

"Several years before Judson bought the theater."

Clara's phone rang, and she answered it quickly. She spoke for a minute, listened, and then hung up. "Let's get to the theater. Adam Harrison wants to meet us there—we need to make a few decisions. Jackson and Brodie just left, investigating the death of the poor woman they found on the decorated lawn of that mansion yesterday. But Adam assured me the place is still crawling with cops. Oh—or I can leave you here, if you'd rather?"

Kody smiled at that. "Neither of us is really kick-ass. We could use Sophie Manning, my almost-sister-in-law. She was a cop."

"We'll draw on her if we need to," Clara said. "For now, I do think we should stick together."

"Yes, that's fine. Now that I have a name, I can work on the computer. Clues to follow. We'll head to the theater."

"You really think something happened there that no one knows about—that someone was murdered there, and it was covered up? Seriously, whether it was done to him by some other hand or not, Brent was higher than a kite on stage—and you did pull it out of the fire."

Kody blushed. "Thanks. I think Brent could have been suggestible. And he might have been fed those lines."

They left the library and headed to the theater. It was after they'd found parking and started to walk the few blocks to the entrance that Kody suddenly stopped cold, a shop window drawing her attention.

Halloween was being transferred into fall and Thanksgiving. Pumpkins and multi-colored leaves were artistically spread about. A small cornfield had been created and a Pilgrim couple stood together at the far side of the window. The wife was holding a pottery bowl filled with ears of corn and other vegetables. She and her husband smiled, looking out over the bounty of their fields—where, Kody saw, a life-sized scarecrow provided protection.

The scarecrow would have scared anything—any bird, no matter how big—with any sense. He was supposed to be a seventeenth-century scarecrow, so he was dressed in a loose white cotton shirt, breeches, and boots. His head appeared to have been fashioned by sliding a burlap bag over a pumpkin, or some other such-sized object. The eyes were buttons and the mouth was leering.

"There you go—Thanksgiving," Clara said. She walked on by the window.

Kody didn't know why she paused, but she did.

The scarecrow was creepy—ridiculously creepy for a display window for Thanksgiving.

"Halloween is over," she murmured under her breath.

Then the scarecrow moved. It turned and looked at her, jumped off its wooden frame, leaned against the glass, looked at her and pointed with its straw arms.

"Clara!" she called.

She wasn't terrified, but she was as frozen inside as she had been seeing the dancer in the death's head mask.

She was angry—and determined.

She raced to the store, throwing open the door, pushing past several women who were leaving, and racing to her left and to the sheet drawn "tapestry" that covered the rear of the display.

"Miss!" a clerk called out, coming quickly toward her.

Kody didn't hear. She reached out to jerk the tapestry aside.

* * * *

"You know how early everything starts for Halloween—theme parks, stores, everything and everyone!" Vickie Bostwick, a curator for the museum, told them.

Bostwick was in her mid-thirties, with short brown hair, thin-rimmed glasses, and a no-nonsense manner. "I didn't think anything of it—we had a lot of 'living statues' out on the lawn, and over several days, many of them were presidents. There were at least five George Washingtons, some Tricky Dickies, and naturally several Lincolns. When I saw the man in the mask dancing on the steps, I didn't think anything about it. Halloween—as I said. Well, it was before Halloween, but everyone goes crazy all October, so it seems."

"What made you think this costumed character had something to do with Miss Oldman's disappearance?" Jackson asked her.

"When I saw the information about the murder—and the picture of her and her dog on the news—I couldn't help but call because *she followed him*. He was doing some crazy kind of stuff with his dancing, and beckoning people. He had a small crowd and they were laughing and imitating his dance steps…Some people walked away, but a few of them followed him. I was just leaving—walking over to the metro station. When I got there, I noticed that two or three people were still following him over to the side street—by the station where I was going—and I think he got into some kind of a vehicle. There were only a couple of girls with him then, but I swear, that poor young lady—Miss Oldman—was with them."

Jackson thanked her.

"I wish I could tell you more," she said. "I…I almost didn't call. I mean, I realize I didn't give you much of anything—other than suggesting that she was kidnapped by Abraham Lincoln."

"No, thank you—we very much appreciate you calling in," Brodie told her and they left. Out on the museum steps, he looked around. The Smithsonian was fantastic—truly what could be considered one of the country's greatest treasures. From their vantage point, he could see The Castle, and he smiled inwardly, thinking of the last time he'd been there.

He'd been with Kody, right after they'd packed up, left Key West, and come north so that he could "consult" until the next Academy class, go through it, and join the Krewe.

Kody had known all about the museum. She'd told him that James Smithson—who had left his estate for the founding of the museum—was interred in his crypt on the ground floor of The Castle. He'd been born a bastard, Kody had said, and since he'd been an Englishman, she believed that it had been his belief in democratic principles that had led him to bequeath his estate to the museum. Construction of The Castle had begun in 1849 and the doors had opened in 1855. Now there were nineteen museums and more auxiliary buildings and…

"So it seems our dancing killer went from being Abraham Lincoln to a death's head," Jackson said.

"A dancing Lincoln," Brodie agreed. "And a dancing death's head." He looked at Jackson. "Somehow, what we've learned, whoever our person is—they have something to do with the theater. I suggest we get back there."

Jackson started to answer him but then his phone rang, and he answered it quickly. When he completed his conversation, he turned to

Brodie.

"That was Detective Hilton. The teams have finished up at the theater."

"And?"

"You know how it goes. They've collected a few items. Hilton says they didn't find any trace of any kind of drug—other than someone's aspirin—anywhere in the dressing rooms, prop, set room— any rooms. Except for Brent Myerson's dressing room. Then again, someone could have cleaned up really well. They have some items they'll test, but you know how it goes with labs. That could take some time."

"I say we go back there," Brodie told him. "I can't help but think the answers are there—somewhere. With someone associated with the theater."

"Who?" Jackson asked. "It could be Brent—he could be an incredible liar. I've seen accountants be incredible liars, and Brent is an actor. A damned good one."

"I guess it depends on how you look at it."

"Acting is, in a way, lying."

"Ah, but some introverts make great actors—and some actors make lousy liars when it comes to reality instead of fantasy."

"You don't think it was Brent?" Jackson asked flatly.

"No, I really don't. Now, he thought it could have been someone who wanted a job at the theater—and wasn't cast in the shows," Brodie said. "I don't agree with that. I sincerely think our man—our woman—who seems to have a talent with drugs, spiked Brent's tea, and killed our Miss Oldham—is an insider."

"If not Brent—Barry?"

"No. I think that Barry never made it out of Brent's dressing room. I think he was passed out—and our killer took his place. He was always hidden—by the mask and by the set. And being behind the curtain, he could easily slip backstage along with anyone else with the right to be there."

"So, still, who? Ginny—who served the tea?"

Brodie shrugged. "Someone who hates the theater, or..." He paused, frowning.

"What?"

"Someone who had a grudge against the theater—or against

Kody."

"Kody is new to the theater—new to the entire D.C. area. And, as far as I know, she didn't have any enemies back in Key West who would have followed her here," Jackson said. "Or do you know of something or someone?"

Brodie shook his head, frustrated. "No—people love Kody. She's supportive of others…and she could have been so many very bad things. Her dad was a huge rock star at one time. She could have been a spoiled brat. She grew up just the opposite." He looked at Jackson and shook his head in frustration. "Let's just get back to the theater. She and Clara might have found something out."

"We're all over the place, you know. Dancing Lincoln, dancing death's head. The theater, a dead girl on Halloween, a drugged actor…and Kody."

"Maybe he was practicing," Brodie said.

"Practicing—as a dancing Lincoln, luring, drugging, kidnapping and then killing a young woman on Halloween?"

"Farfetched," Brodie said. "But…it's there. Somewhere. The connection is there—and that's exactly why the dancing death's head was out in front of the theater."

"To unnerve Kody?"

"She was the one threatened on stage."

"All right, I'm going to get Angela started—we'll see if anyone connected to the theater has roots that go back to the past at the theater—or if they have any kind of a past that might connect them to Kody. I'll tell her it's a priority—and we believe it might connect to the murder of Helena Oldham and the disappearance of the other girls."

"Perfect, thanks. I know Kody is researching the theater now."

Jackson paused to make his phone call to Angela, his wife, Krewe member, special agent—and magician when it came to computer records.

Brodie decided it would be a good time for him to put a call through to Kody.

Her phone rang and rang. He dialed again, and it rang and rang a second time, and went to her voicemail.

He didn't leave a message.

He called Clara's phone instead.

"Hey, is everything all right?" he asked when she answered. "I'm trying to reach Kody, and her phone is going straight to voice mail."

Clara sounded breathless. "It's because she's racing after a scarecrow."

"What?"

"There was a scarecrow in a window display and...Kody burst into the store. The scarecrow disappeared. Kody went after it and"— she paused to gasp in a breath—"and I'm chasing after Kody. I think the scarecrow is gone—pretty sure it escaped."

"Where are you?" Brodie asked anxiously.

"By the theater...maybe a block."

"Jackson and I are on the way."

"Yeah...Adam is already at the theater."

"Get Kody—and get there. Please."

"Yep. That's what I'm trying to do," Clara told him.

A greater sense of urgency began to fill Brodie. "We have to go— now," he said. "And hurry."

Words had begun to spin in his head; an unwelcome memory.

The words spoken by Brent on stage—as the monster he had created of himself.

Spoken to Kody.

You, too, will die in a pool of blood.

Chapter 9

"Miss!"

Kody could hear the clerk calling out to her but she didn't care.

She'd knocked the entire drape down and made a bit of a mess for someone to have to clean up.

But so had the scarecrow.

Who the hell was it? Who in God's name would be out to get her—or Brent? Or destroy Adam's theater? It made no sense.

The scarecrow was out of the window, and though she might not have been the toughest woman on Earth, she didn't believe the scarecrow would hurt her—not in the middle of a store.

And while darkness was coming, there was still light in the sky. The streets were filled with people—it was Washington, D.C., for God's sake—busy, busy, busy. People coming and going and the workday at an end...

"Kody!"

It was Clara calling after her. But Kody didn't respond.

The scarecrow hadn't run for the front door. It had headed for the back. There had to be a delivery door back there.

Clara, of course, was racing after her.

Kody barely noticed. She almost knocked over a spinning rack of tank tops. She pushed onward, running through aisles that advertised "Halloween sweaters, half off!"

And onward.

She plowed into a heavyset woman who swore at her vociferously.

Kody apologized as she ran—barely aware that Clara, too, flew into the woman, and there was more swearing—and more apologizing.

She raced to the back, where there were fitting rooms with a clerk at a little desk outside, seated where she could oversee what went in and what went out.

"The scarecrow—where did the scarecrow go?" Kody demanded.

The clerk's brows shot up in surprise. Kody was afraid she was going to say that there was no scarecrow.

"Uh—that way," the clerk said, pointing to Kody's right.

The directions led to the rear door—and an alley.

It was stupid—incredibly stupid. But she couldn't let the scarecrow go. The dancer in the death's head mask had disappeared.

A girl had died, Brent had been drugged, and Barry had been left half-dead.

She couldn't let the scarecrow go.

Kody burst out of the store and into the back alley.

The scarecrow was gone. She stood dead still, looking around.

But all she could see was the store's dumpsters. The alley was narrow—long, but narrow. And still, all she could see down the length of it was more dumpsters.

D.C. was old. There had been no cars when most of these buildings had been built. Dumpsters were on wheels to be brought to the end of each street when it was time for pickup.

She winced. The scarecrow could have run into the back of several establishments—or run to the end of the alley.

She felt something slam behind her and she started to scream.

"Kody!"

It was Clara, who had been tearing after her so quickly she had collided straight into her back. Clara, gasping, choking, and trying to apologize.

"No, no, Clara, it was me—I'm so sorry. I just…that damned scarecrow is our death's head—I know it. And I let it get away. It was there—right there."

"We can call Jackson. He can get the Krewe and cops out and they can do a door-to-door canvas," Clara suggested.

"For what? He's gone. I missed him—and he's gone," Kody said.

"Okay, we're right down the street from the theater. Adam will be there—and some cops or tech people, and maybe some of our group. We'll tell them about the scarecrow. See what they say—and what we can do."

There was a plastic bottle on the ground. Kody kicked it with annoyance.

"He'll come back as a giant turkey next time. Thanksgiving—we're heading to Thanksgiving, and Brent said on stage someone else would die in a pool of blood. And I could have caught the damned scarecrow—and ended it!"

"Come on, let's head back," Clara said.

Kody nodded, but as Clara walked away, she paused, looking around again, fiercely annoyed with herself.

Her phone rang and she dug in her bag for it.

It was Brodie. Wincing, she answered, trying to sound cheerful—and not breathless.

"Hey."

"Kody, don't go chasing scarecrows."

"Don't worry, he's gone. Long gone."

"He'll show up again," Brodie told her quietly. "And you shouldn't be going after him. Let someone with training—and a gun—do that."

"Brodie, he's going to kill someone else."

"We'll stop him. And yes, we need to do it quickly. We—not you. Kody, we have leagues of police and agents. *You* don't need to find him. We do. I believe he intends to kill again. Two young women are still missing—possibly dead already. But if this is all connected...I'm afraid the someone else he really wants to kill may wind up being you."

"I just became involved in theater. Why me? But please, Brodie, I'm on to something. I think I found our man who died in a pool of blood. Before Judson Newby bought the theater, it was owned by a man named Bainbridge. Bainbridge had been a pirate—never caught, never arrested. There was a rumor he had sunk a ship—and been injured. The theater went to Newby and he took it over, and it was going to be Caroline's theater—she would be the reigning diva. But if Bainbridge was just injured, he might have come back. I know I'm speculating, theorizing, but what if Bainbridge came back, furious about his losses? And he killed Judson and Caroline...and someone killed him in turn? Maybe not right then, but..."

"Kody, will you please get to the theater? Jackson and I are on the way."

"Yes, we're going. Clara and I are on the way, too. Promise. See you there."

"Dakota, wait," Brodie said.

"What?"

"I'm curious—think back. At any time, did you have any enemies I might not know about?"

"Me? Brodie—this has to do with the theater."

"You were the one threatened."

"You were with me down in Key West. My friend and another man were murdered—but we learned why and brought the wretched killer down. No, I'm a nice person, seriously. I think you know that. You met my friends, the people I know down there—nice people. I—"

"What about your dad?"

"My dad? My dad has been dead for years, Brodie."

"But did he have any enemies?"

"I'm sure that, through the years, my father made a few. He was an addict until he met my mom. And he was a rock star. Sure, there had to be people who didn't like him—probably people he insulted. But he's been dead for years."

"Okay. Just get to the theater. I think your man has dressed up as Abraham Lincoln, the death's head, and now a scarecrow. Just get out of there. Get to the theater. We don't have a real face or a real name, but he'll show himself again. We'll get him. Jackson and I are almost there. Clara is with you, right?"

Clara was waiting for her just inside the shop.

"Yes."

"Okay, come on, please."

"On our way," Kody said.

She hung and slid her phone into her bag. She started to turn, and that's when she saw him.

He sprang out of the dumpster as if he were part of a jack-in-the-box rather than a scarecrow. And he was behind her, jumping upon her with a vengeance—a needle in his hand.

She felt it pierce her skin.

She felt the asphalt as she landed hard on it. Felt a thunder of pain in her head as her skull hit hard.

And then she felt no more.

* * * *

Brodie ended his call with Kody and looked over at Jackson. "Kody was chasing a scarecrow."

"A scarecrow?"

"Shop-window scarecrow—that came to life. It's disappeared now."

"Lincoln, death's head, scarecrow—what next?" Jackson asked dryly. "They lost him—a good thing, probably, since neither of them is a cop, marshal, or in any other form of law enforcement. Who knows what this guy might carry—as any person or creation he takes on."

"Kody suggested a turkey. Thanksgiving is next," Brodie said without humor. "She and Clara should be at the theater when we get there or soon after. But I'd like to give Angela another call—and see if she can find out more about a man named Bainbridge—he owned the theater before Judson Newby bought it. The theater went down because Bainbridge disappeared—he was supposedly a pirate."

"Lincoln, a death's head, a scarecrow—has this guy appeared as a pirate?"

"No. But Kody thinks our theater ghosts—the ones none of us, including my parents, have seen, didn't die nicely or naturally. She thinks Bainbridge came in and murdered them—and then someone murdered him. In a pool of blood."

"She has one heck of an imagination."

"Imagination—intuition. I think it's worth investigating. Most of what we work on is theory. Before we knew about anything happening, the man dancing in the death's head mask alerted something in her. And now we have a dead woman, Brent was drugged—and we know for a fact something is going on at the theater. Have to go with something."

Jackson glanced over at him, possibly still doubting the connections, but willing to try all avenues. He put in his call, listened for a minute, and handed the phone to Brodie.

"She found something," he said.

"Bainbridge?"

Jackson shook his head.

"A different connection. Or not. But something that might have to do with Kody."

* * * *

"You can hear me, can't you?" the scarecrow whispered.

Kody could hear, but it seemed she couldn't move. She wasn't paralyzed. She wasn't even afraid. The world seemed to be a strange place -- it was as if she was watching a three-D movie without her three-D glasses.

Nothing was right.

She was being carried by a scarecrow. She was dimly aware of the burlap-covered, pumpkin-shaped head, with its face offering a black-slash mouth. And eye-holes.

The eyes...

They glittered, something purely evil within them. They touched on hers.

But...

The way she felt. It was so bizarre. Something deep inside warned her she should be terrified. This was a killer. A killer straight from a horror movie.

But...

She couldn't move, felt lighter than air. She willed her hands to reach up to the head, wanting nothing more than to strip away the mask and see who he was.

She wasn't afraid. And she should have been. But just as she couldn't will her hand to reach to the mask, she couldn't summon what was needed for fear.

"Ah, Dakota McCoy, beloved, precious person! Born into privilege. Some of us have talent—you must have seen my talent. Some of us have privilege. Ah yes, child of an addict, walking the straight and narrow. Above the earth—every opportunity opened to you. But you just had to open a museum. You didn't need talent. You didn't need anything at all—just being you was enough. I could almost bear it—knowing you existed. But then...you came here."

She knew she was drugged, but since she was, she just couldn't really care. Her one driving desire was to rip the burlap from his head.

She didn't understand where she was going. First, he was walking, and she didn't think they could have walked that far.

Were they in an alley? Was she going to die in an alley—maybe even in a dumpster?

She still couldn't really care. But then, somewhere in her mind, she thought of Brodie. She thought of what they had gone through together, what they had lost—and what they had gained. She thought about the way he looked, his smile, the way he touched her—the wedding they were trying to plan, with blessings from his brothers and friends, and all manner of suggestions from his parents. And how she always smiled, thinking Maeve and Hamish really gave such new meaning to being haunted by one's in-laws.

Would they let her join them? Would she haunt the place with them, watch Brodie go through life, watch...her love, his pain, life, moving on?

Brodie. She loved him and wanted a life with him. She wanted a wedding, a honeymoon, and even their crazy situation with Maeve and Hamish...

As Brodie had told her, they were often busy 'haunting' his brothers, and then again, there was always another show or movie to be seen. The two had their own lives—or after-lives.

She almost smiled at the thought.

And that was good, because her lips twitched.

Fight, fight, fight it, she thought.

If her lips began to move, she could come to where her limbs would begin to move. Her heart was beating; she could hear her heart beating. She was breathing.

And where there was breath, there was life.

She stared up at the scarecrow, determined she would not die.

"You had everything, every opportunity. You were such a damned princess. Always protected, offered everything...and you let it all go. You just let it all go."

It had never been about the theater. But the theater had provided an exceptional platform. His ideas might have been percolating for years, ideas on how to kill and get away with it. And specifically, to kill her and get away with it...

Jealousy and frustration...

"I had talent. I had great talent. And no one would see it. Because I wasn't the child of a great rock star. Michael McCoy wasn't my dad. Michael McCoy..."

Staring up at the scarecrow, she suddenly knew who he was. And she wondered if he had just found out about Timothy Bainbridge...

Or if, somewhere in his twisted mind, he hadn't theorized—as she had—that Bainbridge had killed Judson Newby—and been murdered in turn.

They will find the truth, you know, she longed to say. *They will find you, and you will go to prison for the rest of your life, and rot in the swill of your jealousy and twisted mind.*

She didn't think she could form the words as she wanted them to sound. But that was all right. She didn't want him to know she was regaining the power to move. He could hit her with something again, and then she would die, as he wanted…

She didn't know where they were—her vision was still blurred. She thought she saw all kinds of things and faces around her. Faces…masks.

The death's head mask was there. And she knew.

She was in the theater.

She didn't know how they could be in the theater—they would have had to have gone through the box office area, through the audience, and the stage, and down the stairs…

Unless he had maneuvered the emergency exit? Maneuvered it to open now because he needed it open now. He had never needed it open before, and so, if the police had examined it, they'd have seen that it was locked, the alarm on.

He'd worked it all out. All through the Halloween season. Maybe he'd waited half his life, a decade at least, and when she had come here…

His insanity had been fully fueled.

Yes, he was sick. He had killed before, she was certain. He had then amped up his insanity, perhaps because of Halloween allowing him so much freedom…

He'd killed, but he really wanted her dead.

She suddenly felt herself falling; felt as her body hit an obstruction. Then something was closing over her, and she knew.

She was in the prop room, stuffed into a trunk.

Yes, she was to die.

Somehow.

In a pool of blood.

He was just waiting for the right, theatrical moment.

Chapter 10

Brodie had just entered the theater when Clara called.

"She's gone," Clara told him, her tone hysterical. "I stepped inside while she was just staring around. I thought she was coming right in. When she didn't, I went outside. But she disappeared. I wasn't fifty feet from her—and then she was gone, just gone! Brodie, please, get here—get here quickly. She's gone—the scarecrow took her! Get troops out, get them searching the alley! Everywhere—oh, my God, how did I let this happen?"

"Clara," he heard himself say, "you didn't let this happen."

Jackson was staring at him. Adam had come from the audience out to the box office area. It felt as if his limbs had frozen, as if his blood had gone to ice as well.

But he had to function, and he would function. And he'd find her, he'd find Kody. She was strong, she was a fighter, not an agent. But she was intuitive and...

"He's got Kody. She disappeared from the alley. We need—"

Adam Harrison was on the phone even as he spoke, calling the police and Krewe headquarters.

The area would be flooded and a perimeter would be set. Agents and cops would tear the streets apart.

But this killer had something else in mind. He had been after Kody, but he'd had a connection to the theater, too.

"We need to get going," Jackson told him.

He turned to Jackson, slowly shaking his head. "Let the troops go. We need to stay here."

Neither Adam nor Jackson argued that.

They looked at him. As they did so, Jackson's phone rang.

It was Angela. She must have told him she had something because Jackson put her on speaker.

"Timothy Bainbridge supposedly disappeared at sea, and that was why the theater went into hock and wound up in foreclosure when it was bought by Judson Newby. But I poured through every ancestry site I could find. There is a letter from one of his men up on a site, saying he had been in the city after he was supposedly dead—lost at sea."

"So he might have killed Newby for buying his theater? Someone would have bought it," Jackson said.

"But Newby did buy it. I also found out Bainbridge supposedly left a dozen or so illegitimate children. Seven were adults at the time Newby bought the theater—and died."

Brodie spoke quickly. "So it's possible. Bainbridge came here, bitter, and killed Caroline and Judson. But why would his children have killed him?"

"I don't think they would have killed him. I think someone did, though I don't know who. I'm searching records on any possible relatives or descendants of Caroline and Judson now."

"Did you do any research on Michael McCoy and the Bone Island Boys?" Brodie asked.

"Yes. They had several auditions for back-up singers—they had studio back-up and hired people when they went on tour. Obviously, people were rejected. I'm working on that now, too."

"Thank you—Kody is missing now, Angela," Brodie said.

"I'll get an army on the computers," Angela said flatly. "Go—find her."

She hung up.

"We can get an army in here too," Adam said. "We'll tear the place apart again—"

"No, Adam. Thank you, but no. It has to be us. This killer. He's a performer—a rejected performer. An actor or singer who became…"

"Became a stage hand, or a costumer, or…no."

"Kody…Kody wasn't a performer until she came here."

"No. But she could always sing. Now and then, she got on stage with her dad. She knew what his life had been before he met her mother. She loved singing with him, or with friends of his. But she had her own path in life, things she loved more." Brodie stopped talking. "It has to be just us. And we must move quietly. We have to find him—before his grand performance."

None of them said it.

Her grand performance.

Dying in a pool of blood.

* * * *

Kody waited.

There were good reasons to wait.

First, her would-be killer had to prepare himself. A performer always prepared for the stage.

For her, there would be no costuming or makeup.

Another reason to wait was her fight—a fight she was trying to wage with everything in her—her mind, her limbs, her very cells. She had to will herself to fight the effects of the drug.

How long—how long did she have?

No time. The trunk re-opened and she felt herself being lifted. She'd had her eyes open, and she kept them open. She made a point not to focus on the killer.

She made a point to be limp in his arms.

She wished she could will herself to be heavier, but he was a dancer. He was in prime physical condition.

A talented dancer. How had he come to be so twisted? Had his only audience ever been on the streets? And how was it he had taken those who had loved his work, kidnapped or killed them, kept them somewhere in a drugged and disoriented state?

She stared at him as if she were sightless, but she was not.

She saw his face. He was now dressed up as a Pilgrim—but a Pilgrim wearing the death's head mask. His holidays were all combining.

There was someone at his side. She couldn't see clearly and she almost blinked.

For a moment—one fleeting moment—she saw a woman. A beautiful young woman in a long period dress, her shimmering blond hair swept up with pins.

And she heard the image cry out.

"No, not again. It will not happen again!"

Kody's would-be killer tripped on a step and swore.

But he regained his footing.

They reached the backstage area. He made his way through the curtains.

On stage, he looked out at the audience. "You're here! I know you're here!" he shouted. "Come, see the final performance! You fools—she is talentless, but always offered everything! She is in the right place at the right time! Precious girl, child of the great Michael McCoy!"

The audience area was darkened, but Kody saw Adam Harrison was there. He walked toward the stage.

"About to take a front-row seat? Well, that's just excellent. Is it just you—Deputy Assistant Director Harrison? But of course—I'm sure that fool McFadden is down by the store, tearing dumpsters apart. Well, I have never minded an audience of one. But I also love a show that draws out the tension, don't you, sir? I'd really love for this to be seen by just a few more. And since you don't want to rush the end, you won't rush me—and you won't threaten me. You'll note the musket and knife—excellent costuming. But there is no rubber blade on this knife—and the musket is loaded. Not with blanks—with the real thing."

Adam stood where he was.

Time.

Her captor was playing for time.

He wanted Brodie to see her die.

"I do not intend to rush you, sir. And as for Miss McCoy, you are sadly mistaken in your jealousy. She did nothing to you."

"Oh, sir! I have mulled ways to kill this girl for years and years. And in my wildest imagination, I had not thought she might come here. I had planned ways to strike at an ultimate moment in Key West. I practiced my techniques on others. This…ah, the taste of this is so sweet. I don't mind drawing out the moment at all."

Kody saw the woman again. She was standing behind them and just to the right. There was a man there with her now, a handsome fellow in a Victorian suit with a brocade vest.

"We must stop him, not again, not again, this cannot happen

again!" the woman said.

Her partner tugged at the man holding Kody, all to no avail. "We haven't the strength!" he cried.

Kody knew that yes, indeed, the spirits of Caroline and Judson were haunting the theater.

Maybe she would join them shortly.

* * * *

Brodie and Jackson started from opposite sides of the prep area beneath the stage and the audience. There were half a dozen dressing rooms, costume rooms, prop rooms...

They needed to move swiftly. Time was an enemy now. But if the place began to crawl with police, there would be no chance to save Kody. The killer would either die or be apprehended.

But Kody would die, too.

And they had to stop that stage action from taking place.

Brodie started with Brent's dressing room, nearly tearing it to shreds. Nothing—and no hint of anything. He tried the green room, and then he paused, heading to the hallway to check the emergency door at the back. The door that was always kept locked, only there in case of fire...

Today, it was open. The killer had dressed as a scarecrow, set himself up in the display window at the shop, knowing Kody would come that way to the theater. He had probably even known Clara would be with her. Thankfully, Clara had gone in—the killer might have intended to kill her on the spot.

Only Kody was needed for this performance.

The man had taken her from behind the shop, hurried along the alley and in the background until he'd reached the fire exit. He'd marked his time—leaving it secure for the police search, and only killing the alarm and opening the door today.

The killer must plan on dying along with his last victim. He'd have staged his final performance—but he would have to know that if he hurt Kody, they would gun him down.

Murder—and then suicide by cop. Or agent, in this case.

The killer didn't care about his own life. That made this situation even more dangerous.

His phone started to ring, and he answered it quickly, not wanting the murderer to hear.

But as he did, he heard voices filtering down from above.

The performance had already begun.

"Angela?" he whispered into the phone.

"This seems really sick, but it's all I can find. *The Bone Island Boys* auditioned for a major tour fifteen years ago. They turned down several back-up vocalists and dancers. They were only hiring four for their tour. Among them was a man who had worked as a chorus member, majored in performance at NYU, minored in dance. Ten years ago, he had his name legally changed, and he started working in NYC as a stage hand. Brodie, when he auditioned for the Bone Island Boys, his name was Bainbridge. I think I know your killer—"

"Brodie, come now!"

He was startled by his father's voice. Hamish was standing before him, a look of desperation on his ghostly countenance.

Brodie nodded.

"I know him, too," Brodie said. He hung up and followed his father.

It was time for his own performance to begin.

* * * *

Kody knew she could move. What she didn't know was the right time to move.

When to move to save her life.

The ghost of Judson Newby was still there, accompanied by his Caroline, and he was tugging away at Percy Ainsworth's arms, but to little avail.

Ainsworth felt them, though, she thought.

He kept twitching.

In fact, he was shivering.

Anticipation of what he was about to do—or did he feel the dead tugging at him?

She kept her eyes unfocused, even though Percy Ainsworth was now engaged with Adam.

Adam, of course, was keeping him talking. Tall, dignified, and a handsome man despite his age, Adam had dealt with the worst of humanity many times. He was gifted in a way Ainsworth might not have expected.

Something inside her quickened with hope.

She could see Brodie had come quietly to the stage-right wing. He wasn't alone. Hamish was at his side and Kody realized Maeve had been watching over her.

Percy Ainsworth didn't see the ghosts.

Nor, it seemed, did he see Brodie, weighing the situation from the wings.

Suddenly, Percy Ainsworth went to his knees and deposited her on the floor.

"Late! Where is Brodie McFadden?" he cried out dramatically. "Ah, and there he is!" He turned suddenly, seeing Brodie in the wings.

Brodie…but?

Not the ghosts.

"Ah, sir, and there you are. The great tragedy! Help so close—yet even the most agile, powerful, incredible man could not stop this. Shoot me? I shall collapse upon her with my knife aimed at her heart. Tackle me, and yes, she dies! So relish it, sir—relish this great tragedy. Our beautiful heroine, rendered helpless. The great hero, in the wings, powerless, and then…the death! The death of beauty and innocence!"

Percy Ainsworth stripped away his mask.

He raised his arms, the knife held high—right over Kody's heart.

"Stop him, we must stop him!" Caroline Hartford cried.

"We haven't the strength—" Judson wailed.

"But with us, you might!" Hamish McFadden's ghostly image cried. He and Maeve raced onto the stage.

Percy twisted slightly, gasping, as if he did feel the pull of something on him.

And Brodie took that second. He didn't shoot – the knife might have fallen on her.

Instead, he seemed to fly across the stage.

Ainsworth tried to lower the knife but struggled to do so.

As it came down, Kody used her carefully gathered bit of strength and rolled.

And at the same time, Brodie came down with his flesh and blood power upon Percy Ainsworth, slamming his fist aside with such strength the knife went flying. He then wrestled the musket away from the Pilgrim belt Ainsworth had worn, and it too was sliding across the stage as he wrenched the man to his feet.

"Kill me, kill me, you lackluster coward!" the man screamed. Then, not looking at Brodie, he let out a cry of horror. He was being pummeled from the front, back, and on both sides.

Surrounded by the ghosts of the theater.

All four of them.

"Kill me! God, kill me—get them off. Get them off, make them go away!"

"He's right!" Hamish said, pulling back. "Let him rot in jail. Let him know we exist, that we might visit any time!"

Maeve, Caroline, and Judson also pulled back.

"Kill me!" Ainsworth screamed.

"No, you will rot in jail. After you tell us where your other two victims are stashed!" Brodie roared.

Jackson came running onto the stage to restrain Percy, and Brodie ran to where Kody lay, breathing deeply—focusing at last.

She wanted to hold him so badly.

She still couldn't do that. It didn't matter. He held her. Maeve and Hamish were behind him—they were ghosts, but they seemed to be breathing heavily.

She could only form a few words. Brodie knew she loved him.

She managed something of a smile.

"What great in-laws I'm going to have," she said.

Then she closed her eyes and listened to the sirens, grateful this great tragedy had not had a finale upon the stage.

Epilogue

"Even knowing all that we know," Kody said, "I find it amazing a man could hate me for so many years and wait...and manage what he managed."

Brodie rolled to her. He stretched out an arm, indicating the sky.

It was beautiful. Mauve colors were dancing with golds and crimsons.

It was sunset in Key West. They lay on the beach near Ft. Zachary Taylor. The breeze was soft, the coming night promised to be just right, and for a moment—a precious moment—the world seemed to be perfect.

"Percy Ainsworth—born Richard Timothy Bainbridge—wanted to be a performer. He majored in theater and voice. He had a hang-up on your dad and his band, and he wanted to be a part of it. He was only ever cast as a back-up performer, and from what the shrinks have gathered, he started to snap when he didn't get a job with your dad's band. You must have been there. Maybe your father picked you up, had you sing a few notes...something in him saw you as the enemy."

"I would have been a kid."

"Ah, but the child of Michael McCoy."

"And he just happened to be at the theater?"

"He took jobs at various theaters—in NYC and D.C.," Brodie explained. "He wound up working in stagecraft—and eventually design—because, as he said, it was better than taking a job as a barista. I don't know why things didn't go so well for him, other than that, as we all know, there are only so many roles, so many places for dancers and musicians, and so many talented people who don't get a break. Most of them deal with it. Percy Ainsworth focused his hatred on you." He hesitated. "He's been watching you for years."

Kody shook her head, still amazed someone could harbor that kind of hatred through years and years.

"I think he was so determined you 'die in a pool of blood' that he didn't fix his drug cocktail for you as strong as it should have been. Thank God," Brodie said, dusting sand from her cheek and looking down into her eyes. "Thank God you rolled. I knew I had to do something…but I was afraid. I was so afraid he was right, that…well, we had a lot of spectral help, but…"

Kody reached up, cupped the back of his head, and pulled herself up to kiss his lips. The kiss became deeper than she had intended.

They were on a public beach.

She eased down quickly.

"We need to get a room," he told her.

"We have a room—we have a whole house." She smiled. She'd kept her home in Key West and always would, even if they were mainly living in the D.C. area.

"Time to go there," he said softly and sighed. She knew why.

They had to leave soon because his class at the Academy was about to start. And she had agreed to be in the Christmas play, which she was excited about. Brodie was all right with it—his parents had promised they would be at the theater whenever Kody was working there.

They were becoming fast friends with Caroline and Judson—and working at their skills. All four of them had mastered the "start" button on the coffee machine in the green room.

"Christmas is coming up! A lovely haunted holiday," she said.

He rose and smiled, gathering up their blanket. "You're something, you know. If you hadn't rolled, if we hadn't taken him alive…"

"You found the other two missing girls," she said. "You made him talk—you're going to be such an incredible and very special agent, Mr. McFadden."

He smiled at that. "With you by my side," he said, and kissed her.

The kiss deepened again.

It was a very hot kiss…

A lot of tongue.

A lot of promise for the night to come.

Brodie winced and pulled away.

"You know, we could make your mom happy and get married at the theater," she said.

"Um, we'll talk about it," he said. "For now…"

"Home," she said softly.

He nodded and smiled.

She laughed suddenly.

"What?"

"Well, we're not riding off or anything of the like, but…"

"Yes?"

"We are walking off into the sunset."

"Let's walk quickly, eh?"

And they did.

* * * *

Also from 1001 Dark Nights and Heather Graham, discover Hallow Be The Haunt, Crimson Twilight, When Irish Eyes Are Haunting, All Hallow's Eve, and Blood on the Bayou.

Sign up for the 1001 Dark Nights Newsletter
and be entered to win a Tiffany Key necklace.

There's a contest every month!

Go to www.1001DarkNights.com to subscribe.

As a bonus, all subscribers will receive a free copy of
Discovery Bundle Three
Featuring stories by
Sidney Bristol, Darcy Burke, T. Gephart
Stacey Kennedy, Adriana Locke
JB Salsbury, and Erika Wilde

Discover 1001 Dark Nights Collection Five

Go to www.1001DarkNights.com for more information.

BLAZE ERUPTING by Rebecca Zanetti
Scorpius Syndrome/A Brigade Novella

ROUGH RIDE by Kristen Ashley
A Chaos Novella

HAWKYN by Larissa Ione
A Demonica Underworld Novella

RIDE DIRTY by Laura Kaye
A Raven Riders Novella

ROME'S CHANCE by Joanna Wylde
A Reapers MC Novella

THE MARRIAGE ARRANGEMENT by Jennifer Probst
A Marriage to a Billionaire Novella

SURRENDER by Elisabeth Naughton
A House of Sin Novella

INKED NIGHT by Carrie Ann Ryan
A Montgomery Ink Novella

ENVY by Rachel Van Dyken
An Eagle Elite Novella

PROTECTED by Lexi Blake
A Masters and Mercenaries Novella

THE PRINCE by Jennifer L. Armentrout
A Wicked Novella

PLEASE ME by J. Kenner
A Stark Ever After Novella

WOUND TIGHT by Lorelei James
A Rough Riders/Blacktop Cowboys Novella®

STRONG by Kylie Scott
A Stage Dive Novella

DRAGON NIGHT by Donna Grant
A Dark Kings Novella

TEMPTING BROOKE by Kristen Proby
A Big Sky Novella

HAUNTED BE THE HOLIDAYS by Heather Graham
A Krewe of Hunters Novella

CONTROL by K. Bromberg
An Everyday Heroes Novella

HUNKY HEARTBREAKER by Kendall Ryan
A Whiskey Kisses Novella

THE DARKEST CAPTIVE by Gena Showalter
A Lords of the Underworld Novella

Discover 1001 Dark Nights Collection One

Go to www.1001DarkNights.com for more information.

FOREVER WICKED by Shayla Black
CRIMSON TWILIGHT by Heather Graham
CAPTURED IN SURRENDER by Liliana Hart
SILENT BITE: A SCANGUARDS WEDDING by Tina Folsom
DUNGEON GAMES by Lexi Blake
AZAGOTH by Larissa Ione
NEED YOU NOW by Lisa Renee Jones
SHOW ME, BABY by Cherise Sinclair
ROPED IN by Lorelei James
TEMPTED BY MIDNIGHT by Lara Adrian
THE FLAME by Christopher Rice
CARESS OF DARKNESS by Julie Kenner

Also from 1001 Dark Nights

TAME ME by J. Kenner

Discover 1001 Dark Nights Collection Two

Go to www.1001DarkNights.com for more information.

WICKED WOLF by Carrie Ann Ryan
WHEN IRISH EYES ARE HAUNTING by Heather Graham
EASY WITH YOU by Kristen Proby
MASTER OF FREEDOM by Cherise Sinclair
CARESS OF PLEASURE by Julie Kenner
ADORED by Lexi Blake
HADES by Larissa Ione
RAVAGED by Elisabeth Naughton
DREAM OF YOU by Jennifer L. Armentrout
STRIPPED DOWN by Lorelei James
RAGE/KILLIAN by Alexandra Ivy/Laura Wright
DRAGON KING by Donna Grant
PURE WICKED by Shayla Black
HARD AS STEEL by Laura Kaye
STROKE OF MIDNIGHT by Lara Adrian
ALL HALLOWS EVE by Heather Graham
KISS THE FLAME by Christopher Rice
DARING HER LOVE by Melissa Foster
TEASED by Rebecca Zanetti
THE PROMISE OF SURRENDER by Liliana Hart

Also from 1001 Dark Nights

THE SURRENDER GATE By Christopher Rice
SERVICING THE TARGET By Cherise Sinclair

Discover 1001 Dark Nights Collection Three

Go to www.1001DarkNights.com for more information.

HIDDEN INK by Carrie Ann Ryan
BLOOD ON THE BAYOU by Heather Graham
SEARCHING FOR MINE by Jennifer Probst
DANCE OF DESIRE by Christopher Rice
ROUGH RHYTHM by Tessa Bailey
DEVOTED by Lexi Blake
Z by Larissa Ione
FALLING UNDER YOU by Laurelin Paige
EASY FOR KEEPS by Kristen Proby
UNCHAINED by Elisabeth Naughton
HARD TO SERVE by Laura Kaye
DRAGON FEVER by Donna Grant
KAYDEN/SIMON by Alexandra Ivy/Laura Wright
STRUNG UP by Lorelei James
MIDNIGHT UNTAMED by Lara Adrian
TRICKED by Rebecca Zanetti
DIRTY WICKED by Shayla Black
THE ONLY ONE by Lauren Blakely
SWEET SURRENDER by Liliana Hart

Discover 1001 Dark Nights Collection Four

Go to www.1001DarkNights.com for more information.

ROCK CHICK REAWAKENING by Kristen Ashley
ADORING INK by Carrie Ann Ryan
SWEET RIVALRY by K. Bromberg
SHADE'S LADY by Joanna Wylde
RAZR by Larissa Ione
ARRANGED by Lexi Blake
TANGLED by Rebecca Zanetti
HOLD ME by J. Kenner
SOMEHOW, SOME WAY by Jennifer Probst
TOO CLOSE TO CALL by Tessa Bailey
HUNTED by Elisabeth Naughton
EYES ON YOU by Laura Kaye
BLADE by Alexandra Ivy/Laura Wright
DRAGON BURN by Donna Grant
TRIPPED OUT by Lorelei James
STUD FINDER by Lauren Blakely
MIDNIGHT UNLEASHED by Lara Adrian
HALLOW BE THE HAUNT by Heather Graham
DIRTY FILTHY FIX by Laurelin Paige
THE BED MATE by Kendall Ryan
PRINCE ROMAN by CD Reiss
NO RESERVATIONS by Kristen Proby
DAWN OF SURRENDER by Liliana Hart

Also from 1001 Dark Nights

Tempt Me by J. Kenner

About Heather Graham

New York Times and USA Today bestselling author, Heather Graham, majored in theater arts at the University of South Florida. After a stint of several years in dinner theater, back-up vocals, and bartending, she stayed home after the birth of her third child and began to write. Her first book was with Dell, and since then, she has written over two hundred novels and novellas including category, suspense, historical romance, vampire fiction, time travel, occult and Christmas family fare.

She is pleased to have been published in approximately twenty-five languages. She has written over 200 novels and has 60 million books in print. She has been honored with awards from booksellers and writers' organizations for excellence in her work, and she is also proud to be a recipient of the Silver Bullet from Thriller Writers and was also awarded the prestigious Thriller Master in 2016. She is also a recipient of the Lifetime Achievement Award from RWA. Heather has had books selected for the Doubleday Book Club and the Literary Guild, and has been quoted, interviewed, or featured in such publications as The Nation, Redbook, Mystery Book Club, People and USA Today and appeared on many newscasts including Today, Entertainment Tonight and local television.

Heather loves travel and anything that has to do with the water, and is a certified scuba diver. She also loves ballroom dancing. Each year she hosts the Vampire Ball and Dinner theater at the RT convention raising money for the Pediatric Aids Society and in 2006 she hosted the first Writers for New Orleans Workshop to benefit the stricken Gulf Region. She is also the founder of "The Slush Pile Players," presenting something that's "almost like entertainment" for various conferences and benefits. Married since high school graduation and the mother of five, her greatest love in life remains her family, but she also believes her career has been an incredible gift, and she is grateful every day to be doing something that she loves so very much for a living.

Discover More Heather Graham

Hallow Be the Haunt: A Krewe of Hunters Novella

Years ago, Jake Mallory fell in love all over again with Ashley Donegal—while he and the Krewe were investigating a murder that replicated a horrible Civil War death at her family's Donegal Plantation.

Now, Ashley and Jake are back—planning for their wedding, which will take place the following month at Donegal Plantation, her beautiful old antebellum home.

But Halloween is approaching and Ashley is haunted by a ghost warning her of deaths about to come in the city of New Orleans, deaths caused by the same murderer who stole the life of the beautiful ghost haunting her dreams night after night.

At first, Jake is afraid that returning home has simply awakened some of the fear of the past…

But as Ashley's nightmares continue, a body count begins to accrue in the city…

And it's suddenly a race to stop a killer before Hallow's Eve comes to a crashing end, with dozens more lives at stake, not to mention heart, soul, and life for Jake and Ashley themselves.

* * * *

Crimson Twilight: A Krewe of Hunters Novella

It's a happy time for Sloan Trent and Jane Everett. What could be happier than the event of their wedding? Their Krewe friends will all be there and the event will take place in a medieval castle transported brick by brick to the New England coast. Everyone is festive and thrilled... until the priest turns up dead just hours before the nuptials. Jane and Sloan must find the truth behind the man and the murder-- the secrets of the living and the dead--before they find themselves bound for eternity--not in wedded bliss but in the darkness of an historical wrong and their own brutal deaths.

When Irish Eyes Are Haunting: A Krewe of Hunters Novella

Devin Lyle and Craig Rockwell are back, this time to a haunted castle in Ireland where a banshee may have gone wild—or maybe there's a much more rational explanation—one that involves a disgruntled heir, murder, and mayhem, all with that sexy light touch Heather Graham has turned into her trademark style.

All Hallows Eve: A Krewe of Hunters Novella

Salem was a place near and dear to Jenny Duffy and Samuel Hall -- it was where they'd met on a strange and sinister case. They never dreamed that they'd be called back. That history could repeat itself in a most macabre and terrifying fashion. But, then again, it was Salem at Halloween. Seasoned Krewe members, they still find themselves facing the unspeakable horrors in a desperate race to save each other-and perhaps even their very souls.

Blood on the Bayou: A Cafferty & Quinn Novella

It's winter and a chill has settled over the area near New Orleans, finding a stream of blood, a tourist follows it to a dead man, face down in the bayou.

The man has been done in by a vicious beating, so violent that his skull has been crushed in.

It's barely a day before a second victim is found... once again so badly thrashed that the water runs red. The city becomes riddled with fear.

An old family friend comes to Danni Cafferty, telling her that he's terrified, he's certain that he's received a message from the Blood Bayou killer--It's your turn to pay, blood on the bayou.

Cafferty and Quinn quickly become involved, and--as they all begin to realize that a gruesome local history is being repeated--they find themselves in a fight to save not just a friend, but, perhaps, their very own lives.

On behalf of 1001 Dark Nights,

Liz Berry and M.J. Rose would like to thank ~

Steve Berry
Doug Scofield
Kim Guidroz
Jillian Stein
InkSlinger PR
Dan Slater
Asha Hossain
Chris Graham
Fedora Chen
Kasi Alexander
Jessica Johns
Dylan Stockton
Richard Blake
BookTrib After Dark
and Simon Lipskar